CU00530929

TIME AND TIDE

...because the sea has turned up in so many
of my stories, and time puts in its fair share
of appearances too...

TIME AND TIDE

A book of short stories

by

Janet Jones

Watersmeet Publications

This book is dedicated to all my writing group friends who have inspired these stories, and of course to Peter, who gives me the time and encouragement to write.

STORM-TOSSED DREAMS

*This story was awarded second prize in the Yeovil
Literary Competition 2022*

I was nine years old when I first decided I would never marry. I had crept downstairs while it was still dark – I had no idea of the time, but there was a voice coming from the kitchen and for a moment I thought that Mrs Jenkins, who never seemed to talk to anyone except mother, had secretly invited a friend. I pushed open the door – impossible to do so quietly as it shrieked from lack of oil – but there was no sign of our daily help.

Instead, the voice I had heard was calmly and evenly working its way through a list. I curled myself onto a wooden kitchen chair and allowed the sound to wrap itself around me. I had no idea what the man was talking about, but it was as soothing as a warm bath, a feeling of safety, and I wanted it never to end.

At the identical time, Mrs Jenkins returned and the voice ceased. 'What was that?' I asked following behind her as she pulled breakfast bread and eggs, knives and spoons, from various cupboards.

'That's the instructions for the ships,' she said, shooing me out of the way of the breadknife and the pot of honey.

'What ships?' I was an inveterate questioner, much to the family's dismay.

'Oh – all sorts,' she said, then stopped to think, knowing that I would demand more detail. 'Fishing and ...' Her knowledge of sailing, living as we did in the centre of England, was limited. But I was not to be short-changed.

'And what other sorts of ships?' I asked, sensing something momentous in my life.

'Oh, you know – reckless men who fling themselves at so called adventures and then expect others to come and rescue them ... now come on, out of my way, missy – and go and get out of those pyjamas before your mother sees you ...'

The idea of setting off in a boat – or even better, a fully-masted ship – into the unknown, and being spoken to every morning by the man with the honied voice reset my view of life. Who would want to be polishing brass ornaments or fussing over the price of beef, like my mother, when there was the prospect of worlds to conquer?

Every morning after that I would creep downstairs in those dark pre-dawn hours and listen in the awakening kitchen as he went through the list. 'What does he mean by variable 3 or 4 in far south otherwise easterly'?' I pushed Mrs Jenkins to her limit. Gale, I was familiar with, and thundery showers, but "moderate or good occasionally poor" sounded like an unacceptable school report to me.

'Ask your father,' she rattled in exasperation after the third time of asking.

And of course I did. At first he poo-pooed me, picking up his newspaper, hiding behind a cloud of pipe smoke. For one moment I thought he might not know, might burst my vision of him as my personal Encyclopaedia Britannica. But eventually, when he realised I was not going to allow him to read until an answer was produced, he put down his pipe and paper and pulled me to his knee.

'It's a pattern – like a code,' he said. 'Each day they give information to the fishermen …'

'Or the reckless men who fling themselves at adventures …' I added.

'Yes, all those men at sea need information – on the weather, the winds and the rain, whether they should set sail or heave to, strike forth or look for calm harbour.'

Even my father's words were poetic, and I was smitten. He told me that the map was divided into sections, covering the seas around our island, and that each one had a special name – the names the man with the honied voice used, which would tell the fishermen – and yes, the reckless men – which was their piece of weather, their particular worries to concentrate on.

I pulled out the atlas, battered and stained, and pored over the British Isles. Of course, the forecast areas were not there. Father managed to find me a list, and although at that stage I was unable to place them in their rightful sites around the coast, I began to learn them by heart ... 'Dogger, Fisher, German Bight ... Malin, Hebrides'. I managed small bursts, but frequently left out sections, particularly Trafalgar and Biscay, which never seemed to fit. I made assumptions – correctly as it turned out – that 'Thames' would be at the estuary, Portland, Plymouth and Dover alongside their respective land areas. I established where Lundy lay, and even the prospect of visiting that tiny island held me in thrall. Eventually my harassed father found a shipping map in a second-hand bookshop. It was treasure; it was the Rosetta Stone. It set everything in its place, and I began to plan my tour, safe in the knowledge that I would have no annoying husband (for that is how mother often described my father) to dissuade me or get in my way.

By the age of 12, I had decided I would change my name, for who wanted to be plain Jane Wilkins, when I could be Shannon Bailey or even more splendidly, Malin Finisterre. It was a name for pioneering, for going where no other woman had gone before. I spent my days with maps across my lap as I lolled dramatically on the moth-eaten chaise longue I insisted mother shouldn't throw away, planning the route of my exploits throughout the forecast areas. Initially I had thought to start where the daily forecast begins – in Viking, in the sea between Scotland and Norway. I was prepared to withstand attacks from Eric the Red in his Norse longship until I could battle my way through to North and South Utsire and the wonderful fjords of the Norwegian coast. But then I realised that my trip should have a "grand finale". After much atlas consultation it became obvious - the place to start would have to be "Dover". In this way I could work my way through all 17 areas, returning majestically along the Thames, followed by a flotilla of small ships up to Tower Bridge where I would be greeted by His Majesty and granted a damehood.

Despite these future prospects, father insisted I do more school work - otherwise I would be going nowhere, he said. I conceded that he might have a point, and without telling him, started paying more attention in my geography lessons –

which, to be fair to Miss Weatherby, proved to be extremely useful to my cause. If only the same could have been said of mathematics. But then, a few years later, a *real* opportunity presented itself.

Tom Beecham, a friend of my father's, who had heard of my obsession, called one spring evening on our newly installed telephone. As I sat on the stairs I could hear my father. 'Hmmm. Yes. I see. Yes.' And with every other word he would glance across at me.

I was desperate to know the contents of the other end of the conversation. I gradually slid down the remaining steps and inched my way nearer to the hall table which held a bizarre arrangement of tulips, the latest product of my mother's Ikebana evening class. As I closed in, I knocked the table; the whole thing rocked on its base, and both my father and I held our breath.

'Are you still there, old boy?' Tom shouted at the other end of the line.

'Yes, yes.' My father looked perplexed. 'Look – Jane is here now – perhaps it would be easiest if I handed you over – you can explain what you have in mind.'

I grabbed the telephone eagerly. I couldn't believe my luck. Mr Beecham was offering me a place on his boat, taking part in a practice for the Fastnet Race – The Isle of Wight to the Fastnet Rock and back to Plymouth. That would be at least four of the forecast areas covered – and the beginning of my adventuring life.

Of course, the planning is always the most exciting part, I now realise. But I can't pretend that I wasn't just a jot disappointed when I climbed backwards down into the galley and saw what would be my sleeping quarters. It was effectively the gap between the deck and the bottom of the boat (or keel, as us sailors call it) and had to be slid into horizontally, so that I felt like the filling in a non-too-flavoursome sandwich. The washing facilities proved equally basic, and I decided, before we had even cast off, that I would remain salt-coated and unsavoury until we arrived back in Plymouth.

– I can tell you now - those of you who are not sailors - that the most enjoyable parts of a sea trip are those moments when you are leaving port and then arriving at your destination's similar facilities. There is a period of maybe 15 minutes when the water is calm and the wind is sheltered, when you are gliding gently through small lapping waves. After that, as soon as you turn into open sea, it is like being held upside down on a roller coaster … for hours and days.

By the time we reached the Fastnet Rock I really didn't care that it was considered 'Ireland's teardrop' – I couldn't even bear to take a glimpse; I didn't give a damn whether Drake had been playing bowls at Plymouth while the Armada was fast approaching. All I wanted was to stand on something which wasn't moving and not to be possessed by a gremlin throwing food back out of my stomach only five seconds after it had arrived. And frankly, I concluded that the Vikings were over-rated ….

I write this as I sit at the kitchen table, having finished buffing every piece of brass, polishing the dining room chairs, and copying mother's shopping list into the red notebook which will go to Mr Pearce the grocer, for delivery. Mrs Jenkins has left on the wireless, but I will be ready to flick the switch, just in case the honied voice of the shipping forecast begins.

The newspaper is sitting on the table, still pristine in its folds without father there to re-arrange it, he and mother having – unwisely in my view - taken a trip to the Norwegian Fjords.

I pull it towards me and wander through the pages. I soon tire of political headlines and commentary on the state of the nation's finances, but there, at the bottom of page 4 is a small article about women who have taken up flying.

Wingwalking, to be precise.

As I gaze at the image of them, dancing on the wings of a bi-plane, the thought begins to trickle through my mind that perhaps – just perhaps –

there are bigger choices to be taken than Bully Beef or brawn for lunch; that there might after all be more to life than Brasso and Blue Bags and beeswax polish.

A MOUNTAIN TO CLIMB

Worst of all is the white coat and the blue nurse, sending words back and forth in a tennis match over my head, and me unable to cheer the winning shot.

'I *am* here…' I try to say, but my outburst batters against my cheeks, pinballing around my head, but never finding its way onto my lips. My words and my body feel like they're encased in cement –wrong word – right word won't come – white stuff, hard. Whatever it is, it's holding my hand and my arm and my leg and most of my head in a vice, and there's no way to make these medical people listen.

Something is pulling at my good arm. I force open my eyes, and there's Tom – talking *to* me, not over me. He holds out a hand, intent on shaking mine. I can't make it move, not even a twitch, but he lifts it from the blue blanket and shakes it with the vigour of a deal-maker.

'Skiving as usual,' he says, plonking himself on the bed. 'Windsor half-marathon on Sunday – you up for it?' He is the first to make me laugh, but I can see in his eyes that my smile is sliding off my face, and try as I might, I can't drag it back.

'Seriously though,' he goes on, 'We've got places for The Himalayan. E-mail came yesterday, while you were pratting about in the street, getting saved by strangers.' Only Tom could get away with describing a street collapse, apparently caused by a stroke, to be "pratting about". Himalayan is something we were presumably going to do - that much I get. At this minute though I can't recall anything more.

'Come on mate, you're not getting out of it by pretending you're injured.' Tom stands up. 'You've got six months, so better start training.' He laughs, gives my arm a friendly punch, and blows a kiss to the nurse as he leaves.

Marie comes. She kisses my good side, then my bad, turning when she thinks I can't see, sweeping away a downpour of tears. She tells me the news like she's Sophie Raworth - the serious bits first, and then the feelgood stuff, but it's all just words and none of it sticks. The pinball is rattling in my head again, and my words are still not making it to my lips. But then, as Marie tries to help them through, a single word emerges. To me it's obvious – "laptop", that's what I'm trying to say. What she receives might have come down the string of a tin-can phone, by the look on her face. She pushes an ear nearer to my mouth, and I want to forget about the word and kiss her, but that's not happening either. She takes hold of my hand and looks me in the eye. 'Try again,' she says, willing that one single word to come back.

'Laptop.' It's as clear as daylight in my own head, and I'm proud of myself – not just for getting the word out, but for even remembering the right term. But still it gets lost in translation. It's only by me wiggling the fingers of my good hand that she moves from "itching" to "piano" and eventually to "keyboard". She screams at such a pitch of success that the whole ward turns to see what they're missing. But we're both wrapped up in the ecstasy of successful communication.

Once the machine is sitting there on my lap, I am of course banjaxed for anything I want to say. But Tom saves the day. He bounces in, waving to anyone who will look him in the eye, saying 'Dexterity, that's the job. Get the fingers started and the rest of the body will follow.'

In my head I tell him that this isn't the start of my training for the Himalayan - just a way of stopping myself from being drowned by all the words building up in my head. All that emerges into the stale air of the ward is 'need to speak', and I'm not sure even that is as clear as I want to believe.

Oblivious, Tom produces papers from his pocket. There, shimmering in front of me, is the most stunning picture of Annapurna, sitting amongst her sisters in the Himalayas. I can't stop the tears from pouring down my cheeks. This was to have been it – the pinnacle of our 'extreme triathlons' – The Himalayan Rush - and a visit to Nepal, which to me was the ultimate journey on my bucket list. Now that list is in tatters, taken by some cruel god, laughing insanely as he rips my dreams to shreds.

'Okay,' says Tom, 'Maybe a bit ambitious for our first outing, post pratting-about incident.' He scrambles amongst the crumpled paperwork. 'But here I have just the thing.' Another poster is presented – no colour this time, just Ariel font on white paper, announcing the Taubridge Miniathlon. '6.2 mile bike, one and a half mile run and a piddling quarter mile swim – even your Auntie Mary could do that.'

I look at the greyhound of a man sitting on my bed. He'd only just be getting into his stride on a six-mile bike ride, but his enthusiasm for my recovery is overwhelming. Yet I'm still struggling to lift my hand an inch from the bedclothes.

'It's okay – I've checked with Nurse Patience,' he says, turning to wave to the beautiful

Caribbean face beaming at us. 'She says we can start training straight away.'

Every muscle – every one that I can feel at least – is tensing to resist. From behind the curtain, like a pantomime genie, an exercise person appears. She gives me a squash ball to squeeze in my useless hand. It runs away at my first attempt, but she patiently replaces it, six times, while Tom looks on, beaming at his protégé.

With no mercy, Tom, Marie, Patience and Julia (the 'phys' - my best attempt at her title) put me through my paces, never allowing me to forgo a single handshake, a transfer to a chair, three steps, twenty, or any attempt to hold a piece of paper, which proves to be the most challenging of them all.

I can feel the wetness of tears on my cheeks every day – sometimes frustration, sometimes joy, and when Tom produces a medal for my first length of the ward I am as emotional as any Olympian, the national anthem ringing silently in my ears.

It's September now. I'm home, with only an occasional Julia, but with oceans more Marie and an adequate sprinkling of Tom. When he'd first shown me that poster for the Taubridge Miniathlon, I'd been swept up in his enthusiasm. For one small moment I believed that I would get my body moving and do the entire thing. But August had come and gone with no sign of me being able to do anything more than stagger to the end of the road, or wobble, even on a fixed-wheel bike.

I feel like a month-old balloon. My appetite disappears with my eagerness. I hate Tom for building my hopes when he must have known they would be dashed on the rocks of failure. I refuse to see him, making excuse after excuse to stop Marie allowing him over the threshold. I can see the hurt in her eyes, not only on Tom's behalf, but also at my rejection of her own unending efforts. I don't move from my chair and my fledgling muscles begin to fade.

Today though Marie calls from the doorway as she slips on her best coat. 'Your lunch is in the fridge – I won't be back until late.' There is no kiss on my cheek, no treats left on the table by my side. No TV playing, no audio book. Just the ticking of the hall clock.

Boredom is a strange state. For one thing it makes me hungry, and I force myself out of the chair, staggering across the room to the kitchen. I make toast and search for honey, poking in the cupboard with my walking stick. I bring down the whole array of jars and me as well, and we lay helpless on the floor.

I'm not sure how long it is before I hear whistling – and Tom appears in the doorway.

'More pratting about,' he says, picking me out of the sea of stickiness and propping me on a stool while he clears the mess. He checks his watch.

'Just time for that walk along the lane before lunch,' he says, as if that has been the arrangement all along.

Of course, they've cooked it up between them, Tom and Marie. They knew that the tedium of even an hour on my own would get me moving, and Marie had left the door on the latch for Tom. As I collapse on the park bench, exhausted at my surprisingly okay efforts, Tom digs into his pocket and out comes the miniathlon poster.

'Old news Tom,' I sigh. 'I don't need my nose rubbing in my failures.'

But I hadn't taken in the details, that first time he'd shown me – or else he'd strategically held his thumb over that part of the paperwork. Tom has more sensitivity than many might credit him for. As he thrusts it under my nose, I re-read it - all of it. It's actually advertising for next year. And I realise that, unconsciously, I've been holding the paper without it slipping through my fingers. And that my thoughts are less scrambled, and that my limbs are obeying me - most of the time.

I hand the sheet back silently, awkwardly.

'What do you think then mate?' Tom sneaks a look from under his lashes.

I shake my head, shrug. I lurch to a standing position, surveying the scene across the park – a man in a wheelchair takes my attention, parked, facing the lake, while his family play rounders behind him. A few seconds is all it takes.

'Race you to the café,' I shout, getting some speed into my lopsided stride as Tom's belly-laugh resounds from the path behind me.

THE THIRD BOY

The bad news was accompanied by a Bible.

I wanted to spit every curse I'd heard outside the Rose and Crown on a Saturday night, but my mother's head hung in despair, and so I bit them back.

'Why me?' was all I managed, swallowing 'It's not fair' - too childish, even to me.

'It's a tradition.'

'A tradition that Dickens might have included in one of his cheerful little tales?' I snapped. 'It's 1911, for goodness' sake – what right does she have to dictate to us?'

'*She* is the one with the money.' Mother's voice was uncharacteristically raised. 'And she's trying to help. At least this way everyone gets an education – well you boys do anyway.' She paused, taking breath to sure herself up. 'Oldest son goes to university. Second son goes into the Army …' She looked out of the window, unable to face me. 'And third son goes into the Church.'

I did swear then. Robert and Thomas would be alright, but what did I have in common with Victorian vicars and short-sighted curates? 'I don't even believe,' I said, petulance pouting my lips.

'I'm not sure that's one of your aunt's requirements,' she said. 'She'll hand over her money provided we follow the rules.'

I looked at the Bible positioned in the middle of the table. To add to the insult, it wasn't even a smart sleek black one; it was tattered and stained; it looked like a charred house-brick. To touch it would have been to admit defeat.

'What happens to the fourth son?' I asked flippantly. 'Do they get to be a surgeon or a scientist, something actually useful?' The anger was building in me, the rage powering through my veins like a piston engine. 'Maybe I should go the whole hog and become a missionary, or apply to the Vatican. I'm sure there'll be an opening for a hermit. Because I'm never going to have the life I want, am I?' I pushed my way through the door and slammed it hard, trying to ignore the shards of wood which fell from the worn hinges.

I stood outside, breathing heavily, knowing that none of this was my mother's fault, none of it her choice. She was being dragged along as much as we all were. It was just cruel chance that her sister had married money and mother had married debt.

Robert of course was intolerable, sprinkling our meagre helpings of boiled bacon and cabbage with Shakespeare and Aristotle as though he'd been born to it. Thomas strutted around the house, insisting that Annie or Lizzie shine his buttons and boots, thwacking his makeshift swagger stick at any shrub or child which might venture into his path. I was glad to see the back of them.

I was allowed to finish school at least. I walked away with the slip of paper which said I'd completed the required number of days and at the grand age of fourteen awaited my call to theological college.

While I waited, I did everything I could to encourage Annie and Lizzie to read and write. They'd learnt the basics, but had never enjoyed the escapism which books had given me. We tried Black Beauty and Jane Eyre, but had to draw the line at Lorna Doone, which even to my practised eye was dark and impenetrable. For the most part I helped Farmer Weston. I did the things around the house which father should have done, had he not seen fit to leave us for the wild blue yonder of death and paradise (if you believed in all of that, which I did not). I repaired broken windows and door latches as best I could, and stopped up leaks in the roof. I cut down sagging branches and wayward limbs to encourage a better apple harvest, and I planted whatever vegetable seeds I was able to lay my hands on. All of which was more enjoyable than bible stories or questions of morals or ethics, which to me seemed to have already been woven into our lives by our mother, and not therefore in need of re-invention by black-coated clerics.

I tried hard not to think of what was to come. It only served to boil my blood, and ironically, turning me to what my aunt referred to as "the demon drink" – not in any serious quantities, but enough to have mother wittering and worrying that I would forego my chances of salvation and a better education.

One day I returned from Farmer Weston's, hot and bleeding from our efforts to put a new fence around the sheep. My hands were ripped to shreds and mother poured water into a cracked bowl and tried to bathe the dirt from them. As I sat, allowing her to minister to me, I looked across at the table.

'What's that?' I enquired of the large sheet set out beneath my mother's prized fountain pen.

'The Census,' she said, trying to hook a thorn from the pad of my thumb.

'What – as in returning to the town of your birth ....' I went on, recalling Mary and Joseph's return to Bethlehem.

Mother looked up, smiling. 'So, you did pay attention in Sunday School after all,' she joked. 'Maybe theological college won't be so bad after all.'

My good humour was immediately drowned. I had managed for a few hours not to think of my impending fate, but here it was, back in my lap, and hurting as much as the punctured skin.

'I've to list all who will be living here on Sunday,' she went on, ignoring my miserable face. 'I've already made a start.'

I held my hand, wrapped now in torn strips, close to my chest and stepped over to the table, pulling the paper round so that I could see what mother had written. She had recorded herself as head of the household, and had added my own name, but so far had left a space under 'occupation'. As I glanced over I could see that she wished I had already taken up my learning, that she wanted to list me as 'scholar' or 'clergyman' - something of importance. Not as farm labourer, which would sit on the records for eternity.

I went back to the form, scanning mother's neat strong hand. Alongside her own name were columns of figures – number of children born alive, children still living, children who had died.

And there, under that final column, was a bold and definite '1'. I looked up at mother now at the sink, water falling from the single tap into the blackened kettle. My head went from her to the page, back and forth, not understanding what I was seeing. As far as I was aware, there were five children – Robert, Thomas, Annie, Lizzie, and me. But here was another - a fully birthed child, yet no longer with us.

'Who is this?' I asked, as casually as I could.

'What's that my dear?' she said, clattering the kettle onto the stove.

'This – here – this 'child who has died'?'

She slid into her seat at the table, pulling the form round to her own view, looking wistfully. 'That,' she said, quietly, 'Was Henry. He lived for four weeks, but he died of bronchitis. Sweet child,' she said, stroking the sheet where the solitary mark proclaimed his existence.

'But why did you put him on – when he's not here?' Curiosity had overtaken any sensitivity to my mother's feelings, and thoughts were racing through my head. 'And when – when was he born?'

'I have to fill in the form truthfully – it's the law.' Mother looked up at me, the lines of maternal failure crumpling her face. 'And he was born in 1895,' she murmured.

I wasn't sure if her whisper was in reverence to the lost child, or in anticipation of my thoughts;

because my mind was swinging to and fro like a champion conker, counting, calculating, re-ordering the list of children.

'So … he – Henry – would have been older than me?' I asked, aware I was stepping on ghosts.

'Yes,' was all she said, but that solitary word told me she had reached the crux of the story ahead of me.

'So, he was … the third boy, the third son?' The words stumbled from my mouth, hoping I was right, worried I was wrong.

Mother stared at the sheet which recorded the entirety of her family. She didn't speak, didn't move, despite the singing of the kettle. Eventually she nodded, folding her arms against the anticipated barrage from me.

'So – I'm not the third son, and I don't have to go into the Church?' I asked excitedly. 'I can make my own choices?' I whooped and jumped from my chair, spinning round the kitchen.

'Except that Aunt Harriet only funds the first three boys,' she said quietly. 'Nothing after that.'

I stopped in my tracks, slowly absorbing the significance of her words. 'Aunt Harriet doesn't know about Henry?' I was dumbfounded that a sister would not know about a child who had come and gone.

'She went travelling – with her new husband. They were gone for months. I was going to write – but then poor Henry …' Her words faded.

And so, begrudgingly, I took on the burden. I felt better about the whole thing, sensing that I was somehow living a little bit of the life that Henry had missed. And, against my better judgement, it worked out reasonably. I learned the religious craft as I helped minister to soldiers broken by the Great War and eventually found my way back to an everyday life.

I'm writing this now, at the study in the vicarage. A rambling old place, impossible to heat, but a home – and a happy one at that. And I manage to disguise my lack of belief from the clergy, and from the congregations who have come and gone. They seem happy enough that I can perform the required weddings and funerals, that my sermons are bearable, and that I don't pour fire and brimstone over their heads in response to their misdemeanours. And life's game of chance has brought me bounty in the shape of Eliza, my wife, and our four beautiful children. But I won't allow any family traditions to darken the days of *our* sons – especially Henry, our own third boy.

ON THE BEACH

Mother brings a tray of tea, cups shivering unseasonably in the sunshine as she carries them from the umbrellaed café across the sand. Her purse is sitting alongside, and a little slop from the pot washes her last pound note.

Jennifer wishes that there was no change left from the order, that it had all been spent on ice cream; but she knows this is to be her treat – her end of holiday surprise - and she will act surprised even though she knows it is coming; will dutifully lick her lips at the two scoops - one vanilla, one strawberry - when what she really wants is to have to stand up to eat, because the knickerbocker glory she has chosen is too tall to tackle in any other way. And other children would gather round, watching enviously as she tackles fruit and ice cream and strawberry sauce, until she holds up the final spoonful in triumph.

Mother sinks into the red and white striped deckchair, cup in hand, absorbed in the newspaper world of petty scandal. Jennifer looks around for distraction, hobbles barefoot between rocks and sand to the water, where adventure must surely be waiting. She paddles with her skirt tucked into her knickers, the elastic in her costume having finally given up and no new one forthcoming. It is a balancing act, with feet anchored to the sandy floor, wobbling left and right, daring to move just a little too far to see if the waves will push her over when she's not looking, even though it will lead to a slap on the back of her legs for spoiling her dress. She goes a little deeper and her feet sink to her ankles in the muddy sand. She imagines starfish, darting, wondering which way to go, which is their best foot to put forward and she is sure she can feel little fish nibbling at her toes. They will hate the taste of the Dettoled bath water which mother insists on, which is strong on her skin, and she pictures them pulling faces as they spit the little bits of her out.

She wobbles her way back up the beach, narrowly avoiding a boy with candy floss. Annie told her that it is made of cottonwool, and she knows that cottonwool is for babies and cuts; she would rather the story that it is mermaid's hair, that posses of fish-tailed girls are daily snipping at each other's locks; but she tried it once and it made her teeth squeak, so she will heroically leave the pink hair for the girls to comb beneath the waves.

She squeezes in next to mother's deckchair and begins scooping and zigzagging patterns in the sand, allowing it to pour through her fingers like dried water. The wind is playing on the beach now, and steals the particles from her, throwing them over mother and on to the newspaper with the shouting headlines. Mother clips her head, telling her to leave the sand alone, to move away. She gets up, pulling her skirt from her knickers, wishing she had on the shorts and jumpers worn by the family nearby; they look remarkably like George and Julian and she looks around for the rest of the Famous Five, who are probably at this moment pursuing a vital clue to unlock their next mystery.

Jennifer hunkers down and shuffles herself along a narrow track of sand towards the waterline, leaving a bottom-sized trail in her wake. The grit begins to chafe her skin but still she continues until she is sitting on the wet solid sand at the water's edge. There is spray in the air and it slaps her face and tangles her hair but she doesn't care. She thinks she looks like a madwoman, ready to be locked in someone's attic. She watches as a man comes towards her. He's red-faced, zigzagging like Uncle Tom on a Friday night, and every few paces he stops and sings the next line of his song, gazing out to sea. His rolled-up trousers and bandana make him look like a pirate, Jennifer thinks.

Seagulls are looping the loop around him, adding to the nautical panorama, and she is convinced he will have sailed the Capes, the Oceans and the Spanish Main.

She sees that he has a newspaper bundle under his arm, and the tang of the sour vinegar wafts as he passes her, and she's tempted to see where he goes. She pushes herself up onto her knees, and brushing the sand from her legs as she stands, she glances at her mother, who is still sucking up the headlines through her cats-eye glasses.

The lure of the chips, and an adventure bigger than mother's parsimonious tea tray beckons her like a siren's song. She turns in the direction of the red-faced man.

SOMERSET PRESS
"Jennifer Rowley, aged 11, has been missing now for ten days. She was last

seen on the beach at Anchor Bay,
playing alone.

Her mother says it is completely out
of character for her to wander off.
'She's a very homely girl, not given
to flights of fancy,' Mrs Rowley said.
Police are appealing for witnesses."

GLOVES

Ironically, it was our visits to church where it all started. Every Sunday the same – only the clothes changed. In winter, a matching lilac coat and muff, and a hat knitted by my mother – various shapes, but the preferred (by her at least) was a tammy, plonked on my head and yanked by me to an angle I considered jaunty and sophisticated, and re-arranged by mother, so as not to be blasphemous. But the summer – that was a different question. Crisply pressed summer-best dresses, white socks, white shoes (blancoed by my father to hide the scuffs), a white hat with small brim – and then the gloves. Always gloves.

And so we went, off to church, a quarter mile walk, and with any luck a lift back from my father who might be parked up outside, and my heart would leap at the thought of not having to walk all the way back. I had done my penance already, sitting through those interminable services; they were meaningless enough to an eight-year-old, but when they were in Latin, the monotonous phrases murmured back and forth were like the hum of grumbling bees in my ear. I would sit daydreaming, looking blindly at the prayerbook in front of me - perfectly capable of reading and following the words, but having no interest in what was written there. My mother would, from time to time, snatch the book from me with a sigh, or a tut, or both, rifle through and find the correct page and ram it back into my hands. And the whole process would start again, with me occasionally turning a page when I saw others doing the same. My sister and I had long since been separated, sitting on either side of mother to curtail our antics, so I had to find something else to occupy me. The ping of the bells by the altar boys was a minor entertainment; better was the wafting of incense – a job which I decided was glamorous enough for me to aspire to … if it wasn't for the fact that the pungent odour made me feel faint – an occurrence not approved of by mother, who took it as a sign that I was possessed in some way by evil.

The best distraction of all was the collection plate. It usually came at over the half-way point - and signified that the end was at least in sight. I was fascinated by the assortment of donations which sailed past me. Some were in little brown envelopes – the sort wealthier children brought their school dinner money in; others saw fit to throw a ten-shilling note into the plate, as though it were a mere nothing. To me it was the amount I received from my grandfather for my birthday, and therefore too great a fortune to be given away to some unknown cause. My mother always had coins ready, and as we got older, she would hand us a threepenny piece each, or a couple of pennies, presumably so that we would get used to giving our hard-earned cash away. At first I worried that I would miss the timing and incur the wrath of mother as the money fell to the floor or rolled down the aisle; but then I realised it was possible to clink the already-donated money but still hold on to the coin. The gloves we wore were perfect – not just as a hiding place for the withheld threepenny bit, but also as an enigmatic distraction. It was apparent to me, even at that young age, that people saw the gloves and not the activities of the hands inside. I knew nothing of the technicalities of magic tricks, although I was fascinated by David Nixon, a magician on television, and watched whenever we were allowed. I started to pay more attention, and practised his tantalising hand and finger movements in the mirror whenever I was alone in our shared bedroom.

But then came the day when our excellent white gloves were exchanged. My sister and I were bridesmaids for our aunt and uncle, and as well as the sky-blue satin dresses and accompanying puffed-up petticoats, we were presented with matching chiffon gloves. Initially I loved them – very Audrey Hepburn, another of my fascinations, and the sort of impractical thing that mother would never have bought. I admired my hands, looking at them this way and that through their cobweb covering of blue – which was fine and dandy when you were collecting accolades as an endearing bridesmaid, but of course my frugal mother then insisted that we re-use the gloves every Sunday. They were sheer, almost totally see-through – and therefore unable to conceal the coins which I was regularly rescuing from the collection plate.

I tried creating holes, splits in the seams, but despite their gossamer appearance, the gloves were as tough as a boxer's. Nothing I did had the slightest impact, and so I saw the weeks go past with no financial reward. It was only when, by chance, I realised that the hotter I made my hands, the more the gloves would tighten around my skin, leaving deep red indentations on my swelling fingers; eventually mother conceded and let me return to the white cotton gloves. I returned to the collection plate with added vigour, but also, to my mother's confusion, donned the gloves at any family occasion. I had perfected the art of making coins disappear and reappear - behind granny's ear, or Aunt Molly's hair — enabling me to stash away all manner of donated sweets and sixpences while my aunts and uncles implored me to do "just one more" Christmas trick.

And perhaps it was that which instilled in me a love of "easy" money.

The church visits petered out once my sister and I had completed our Confirmation. It seemed my mother had taken it as her duty to drag us to that point and over the line, but then professed we were "old enough to make our own decisions about church". We needed no encouragement to abandon the 15-minute walk and the interminable Latin murmurings, but the price of freedom was high – no more readily available coins - and so I needed to look for new sources of finance.

A Saturday job seemed likely. After a short stint in a local sweetshop, with the owner always hovering, I moved on to greater things at Marks and Spencer; but they had already anticipated petty pilfering and doled out distinctly unglamorous uniforms with no pockets – and gloves, even back in the late 1960s, were not required uniform for sales staff.

Despite my parents' serious work ethic, hard labour seemed a lot to ask for the sort of pay a person of few qualifications might warrant (those confirmation classes having done nothing to boost my employability); I was considerably more interested in what my father called 'a champagne lifestyle' even if it was on a pale ale income.

I returned to the tricks I'd learnt from David Nixon. I found that I didn't need the white gloves; I could "palm" coins – and even playing cards - without having to think about it; but I was realistic enough to realise that even a mountain of coins wasn't going to make my fortune – and neither was a straight "nine to five" job going to satisfy my lust for glamour.

Then a slice of serendipity came my way. A friend, going on maternity leave, asked if I would cover for her. My work-shy instinct was immediately to say "no", but somewhere in the depths of my brain, bells very like those of the altar boys, began to tinkle. 'Yes,' I said, before I could argue with myself. 'That would be great.' The job, I knew, would be unglamorous, the clients frustrating, and my dreams were suddenly filled with the grubby coats and abandoned false teeth which I was sure must fill her Lost Property office, but that bell kept ringing.

Abigail trained me well - all there was to know about logging and storing and retrieving the most bizarre array of lost property; but it was her parting shot which made that bell ring off its chain. 'Oh, I forgot – pregnancy brain freeze!' she laughed. 'Fridays and Saturdays – you will get a *ridiculous* number of bank cards handed in. People out on the town, totally clueless once they've had a drink or two …'

The woman who handed in the first Mastercard was wearing white gloves, and I worried that it was some sort of sign – the Latin mass come back to haunt me, Catholic guilt and all that. But I took the card, assuring her it would be safe. My colleague, Brian - a fan of the beige anorak - watched conscientiously as I opened the small safe to store the card. He nodded approvingly. 'Well done' he said, as though I had performed CPR and saved a life. I smiled sweetly and returned to the counter. By the end of my shift,

I had been handed six debit cards and two credit cards, which were all now safely stored …

… in the pockets of my jeans.

The palming which I had so successfully learnt and which had made Christmas sixpences and royal flushes disappear, had come to my assistance once more.

I make my first purchases on my way home – before the owners have sobered up enough to realise their bank cards are missing. I call in at Regent Street, where stores are open until late, and purchase three elegant outfits … plus a pair of those Audrey Hepburn "Breakfast at Tiffanys" gloves which I have coveted since I was eight.

FATHER AND THE TRAIN

I hadn't thought of my father's famous maxims in years – although he had spouted them often enough when I was younger. But you have plenty of time to think when you're going nowhere, when four walls are all the scenery you're likely to view for some time, and the conversation I'd overheard at lunch had brought him to mind.

Some old fellow, toothless, had been pointing his plastic fork, stridently insisting to his fellow diner they "shouldn't judge a book by its cover" as they made fun of his wayward looks. It had been a phrase my father had used often, and his sonorous voice in my head took me back to that fateful day on the train.

I had been minding my own business, preferring to be unsociable, and had booked the outside seat in the hope that no-one would bother to push their way through to the window space next to me. It worked for a while, the train being relatively empty as it chugged out of Taunton Station, but as the seats filled and we pulled into Bristol, the gaps gradually filled. A family bundled onto the train at the last moment – elderly parents, and their adult daughter presumably, and proceeded to take over the whole carriage. They had obviously made full use of the M&S on the station concourse, so as well as their collection of suitcases and holdalls they also had a full and varied assortment of carrier bags. It took them what seemed an eternity to settle themselves and their entourage of bags, but once they had, the contents were immediately revealed to the rest of the passengers. Sausage rolls, crisps – lots of crisps, Viennese Whirls, Bakewell slices and iced finger buns, chocolate biscuits and finally fizzy drinks. And believe me, these were a family who were already on the wrong side of obese. But I digress. Not only did they take up more space than their allocated seats and table tops, but they consumed the relative calm of the quiet carriage as voraciously as the food. The remainder of the carriage was treated not only to the cacophony of their munching and their offering of the various treats to each other, but also a running commentary on what they had done whilst in Bristol, and what they might do once they had arrived home.

The patriarch of the group had squeezed in opposite me, and mother and daughter were on the other side of the aisle. The gentleman who they had trapped against that window made eye contact with me several times, raising an eyebrow and shaking his head. He was wearing a smart suit and a rather attractive purple tie, and had the look of someone who wished, too late, that they had booked the first-class carriage. Eventually he wriggled in his cramped seat and declared loudly 'Look, why don't I let your husband sit here, and I'll swap with him … then you can all sit together.' The inference was clear – "so that the rest of us don't have to witness more of your pantomime than is necessary," but he said it so politely that the mother, blinking shortsightedly at him, appeared entranced and had little option but to agree.

Of course, the move was a major challenge of logistics, but eventually they were settled and I was faced with the smartly dressed gentleman. We smiled and nodded, grateful to have distanced ourselves from the family, and when the buffet trolley came through, we bought ourselves overpriced celebratory coffee, and got into polite conversation.

'Off on a business trip?' I asked, indicating his suit and his laptop.

'Well, in a manner of speaking,' he smiled. 'I have my own business – investment portfolios, that sort of thing.'

He said no more, returning to his screen to check the progress of some capital venture no doubt.

Father had quite recently died, and I had been the sole beneficiary of his will. He hadn't left a fortune, but a surprisingly welcome amount nevertheless, and one which needed to earn its keep if it were to maintain me through to my old age. It occurred to me as I swilled the remainder of my coffee in the bottom of the cardboard cup, that this man might be able to help.

'Do you give advice - you know, to average members of the public?' I asked tentatively. 'Although, I suppose you're more up-market than that,' I continued, giving him a let-out if he didn't want to be bothered with a small fish like me.

'No – not at all. I enjoy giving people a step-up to the world of investment,' he said. He opened a brief case and pulled out a brochure. 'Here, take a look at this. Give me a call if you're interested.'

All very fair, it seemed. The brochure was full of enticing examples of clients making fortunes despite their financial inexperience, and, as the train sped its way towards London, I kept him occupied with a string of questions. By the time we arrived at Paddington I was pretty much convinced that this was the opportunity for me, but still he continued to be reasonable.

'Take your time, think it over,' he said. 'Give me a call and we can make absolutely sure it's the right option for you.'

I made my way on the stifling underground to my hotel, and spent the remainder of the evening, after I had eaten, going through the information again. By the following morning I had decided but didn't want to appear too naïve, so waited until the Monday to ring him. He was about to go into a meeting he said – important overseas clients – so asked if he could call me back. There was probably a rat to sniff at, even at this stage in the proceedings, but I was so taken with the idea and the serendipity of our meeting that I was more than happy. When he rang though, he said that he needed to go through paperwork, so it was probably better if we met in person. 'When are you back home?' he asked.

I told him, and he suggested coming to my place on the Friday. 'I've also got another option for you to consider – a new investment we've been trialling on a select group with the intelligence to grasp the finer points, if you take my meaning.'

"Flattery will get you anywhere". That was another one of Dad's favourites, and it proved right. When David Montgomery-Hill – for that was the investment advisor's name – visited, he brought an expensive bottle of white and proceeded to outline what seemed to me the very epitome of sophisticated investment know-how. I went for it, feeling quite the City gent, and handed over almost the full proceeds of my father's estate.

'This gives you a wonderful starting point,' David said, eyeing my newly-signed cheque. 'And if you can get twelve more people signed up as well – well the world's your oyster, as they say.'

I practiced David's sales speak in front of the mirror until I was word-perfect, then launched myself onto the good and the great of Somerset, surprising even myself with the amount of money I hauled in. It wasn't all for me of course, I would need to feed much of it back into the "portfolio", but I was able to keep a decent percentage, and felt quite the business executive as I bought the accoutrements of a financier on my proceeds. Another round of trawling the monied of the

West Country and more bulging pockets; I couldn't believe it was so easy, and spent my evenings calculating how long it would be before I could retire.

All my evenings that is, until that ungracious thudding came to my front door.

Half of Avon and Somerset's finest officers bundled into my hallway, and immediately seized phone and laptop, and every scrap of paperwork from my desk. I was in their van before I could tie my expensive new shoelaces.

But no matter how many beans I spilled, how many times I mentioned Montgomery-Hill's taking of my *own* funds, there was no stopping them. I had defrauded thirty-five people out of their life savings with my pyramid scheme they said, and that was not going to be considered lightly by the judiciary.

And what of the man himself? Well, it appears that this "strangers on a train" routine is one he has undertaken any number of times – and of course the name of Montgomery-Hill has been substituted endlessly, and he, and his own proceeds of crime, are apparently as elusive as the Scarlet Pimpernel himself.

And the family with the cakes and crisps – remember them? They were part of his set-up too it seems. A well-known distraction technique they tell me – and a perfect example of more book covers not to be misjudged.

THE START OF HER

This is based in part on the story of a woman who lived in our house in the late 19th Century

The bolt, slamming across the front door in the otherwise silent house, rammed home all that the day had brought to her. And yet still she climbed the stairs in a daze.

The banister moaned under the weight of her weariness, and as she turned again onto the pinched spiral steps to her attic room, the thought overwhelmed her that there was no-one now to demand or to expect of her. She stopped, listening for a sound which would contradict her thoughts. But there was nothing other than the boards creaking under her tired shoes.

The night was filled with thoughts and dreams, with wakenings and darkness, until morning crept round the faded curtains. Mary Ann glanced at the clock on the otherwise bare bedside table, hurrying to rise, then remembering, and sinking back under the blankets. There was no-one to rise for, no breakfast to be laid, and a hearth which could be cleaned and set at her choosing. She rose nonetheless, then hesitated as she went to fetch hot water. Normally she used the bowl and jug in her room, but now she could wash at the bathroom basin, fill a bath if she chose, or take a dozen towels from the linen cupboard, with no fear of comeback or reprisal.

Miss Sarah had had a sharp tongue in her day, but there was little authority to be given from a sickbed; the mistress had whispered her fading requests and Mary Ann had put them into practice, ensuring the grocer was paid and that the butcher provided their insignificant orders. But now there were no words, harsh or hushed, just the never-ending ticking of the hall clock. For the time being, Mary Ann had no-one to please but herself, yet already she was lost without a pattern to her day.

The only thing, she decided, was to continue as if her mistress were here. She checked the front curtains were respectfully closed, then swept and cleaned and washed, stopping only for tea and a plain biscuit, despite the fact there were fancy ones in the patterned tin on the shelf

A knock came to the black front door. A messenger. With a note, from Mr Scrivener. 'Please attend my offices at your earliest convenience.' Mary Ann knew of the solicitor's rooms – they were a stone's throw from where she stood. But her entry into such premises was unprecedented and troubling.

Her mind jumped to all that he would ask of her – to collect her belongings, to touch nothing of her mistress's, to remove herself from the house forthwith. And she considered, fleetingly, bundling her small collection of belongings and waiting for the coach to take her to Taunton, removing the need for any embarrassment with Mr Scrivener. But she had never been a runaway – she had stuck her place here for … how many years? she asked herself as she once more negotiated the stairs and sought out her cloak and bonnet.

Twenty-five, it had been. Twenty-five years since she had first crossed the threshold and come to work for the family. Then there had been old Mrs Barnes and the other daughter, Grace, as well and she had worked for the three women, with seldom a moment for herself. But first the mother, and then Grace had gone, and she had assisted Miss Sarah to keep the house and themselves going as best they could.

And now there was just her. And not even that for much longer, she thought, as she closed the kitchen door behind her and made her way along the street.

The solicitor's office was stark and chilled, not somewhere to linger she thought, as she gave her name and waited silently to be attended to.

It was not just her mourning clothes, but her whole being which seemed to blend with the dark-wood panelling; so it was no surprise to her that the gentleman in frock coat who emerged from a unnoticed doorway needed to peer over half-moon spectacles to find her.

'Aah, Miss Davis,' he said at last. 'Come this way if you would.'

She followed reluctantly, sure that the stability of the polished wood floor was about to be rocked beneath her feet.

'Take a seat, take a seat.'

His parrot-like words came with no colourful plumage. He looked like a raven, she thought, as he pecked at the papers on his vast desk. She slid onto the upright chair which he indicated and waited for the worst.

'Well, as you may be aware, the deceased, Miss Barnes, has left her affairs in the hands of Scrivener and Cosgrove.' He looked up at her, nodding sagely. She said nothing, not wishing to hasten the inevitable.

'You of course, as her trusty …' He searched for the appropriate description, and Mary Ann thought that she too would have struggled to summarise her position. She had been cook, cleaner, housekeeper, and latterly helpmate …

'Aide.' He settled on. 'You have lived at the property for – how long?' He shuffled through papers, then peered again, making her feel like a scientific specimen.

'Twenty-five years, sir.'

'Indeed, indeed.' He paused. 'And have you no other home – no family place?'

She shook her head, already mentally trudging the streets. His drawn-out questioning prolonged the agony, but she sat in silence, concentrating on the ink stain which had penetrated the grain of his wooden desk.

He rustled papers, cleared his throat. 'Well, it is very fortunate then, Miss Davis, that your employer has seen fit to be particularly generous.' His face said "foolish". 'As you will be aware, there were no children, and, it seems, no other living relative …'

His subsequent words weighed heavier on Mary Ann than any bad news. They pressed on her chest, and were in danger of pushing her to the floor. Mr Scrivener rang a small bell on his desk. The young man from the outer office appeared, and was instructed to bring tea.

'I understand that this will have come as a considerable shock, Miss Davis,' Mr Scrivener spoke as he rang his spoon against his china cup. 'But you are now a woman of property and some considerable wealth.' Another sombre tolling chime of metal against porcelain. 'You must spend time - take stock of your situation. I would suggest that we meet again, within the fortnight, so that I may advise you on your options, as well as your responsibilities …'

Eventually, Mary Ann retraced her steps, stopping now to stare anew at the bold black door — *her* black door. She tentatively slipped the key into the lock, entering the hallway for the first time from the family side. She stood in awe, gazing at the paintings on the wall as though they had appeared in her absence, at the handsome clock, the doors leading to the various rooms. She drifted from one to another, fingering the antimacassars and the cushion tassels; she sat in the visitor's chair in the front parlour.

She continued through the house, seeing things which had long become invisible with familiarity. All hers. She picked up a china ornament – a ragged street-urchin – and placed it inside a cupboard. She had never liked it. She sat at the mistress's desk and opened drawers, ignoring for the moment the paperwork which was now hers to worry over. She took a pen and a sheet of notepaper, considering a letter about her news – but the only people she knew well enough to share it with were the people who no longer lived here. She swallowed the thought, and continued her tour, drawn inevitably to her mistress's room.

Tentatively Mary Ann opened the chest-of-drawers, pulling out camisoles, petticoats, skirts and gloves; she reached to the top shelf of the wardrobe and took down Miss Sarah's best bonnet. She had long coveted it, and now she placed it on her head and observed herself in the mirror as she tied the lilac bow beneath her chin.

She found the matching jacket, and buttoned it down her chest. She would go to the town – not today of course, but when the time was right - and buy a cake which she had not had to make for herself, and flowers from the florist. She would hold her head as the townswomen gawped, and visit the dressmaker and choose and change her mind, and choose again. And perhaps she would find a ... what was the word that Mr Scrivener had used? ... an 'aide' for herself, someone who could worry about the stains on the drawing room rugs, while she sat at the desk and wrote letters; while she planned the confections they would eat when Mrs Partridge and the other grand women came to tea, as they surely would now, if only to be curious. And then of course there was William Adams, the Postmaster; he had always had a soft spot for her ... maybe he too would visit?

GIVING BACK

*This story was a runner-up in an 'Autumn Voices'
short story competition*

The old man studied the cheque, shook his head
… then tore it into miniscule pieces.

'Dad! What the hell are you doing? Stop!'

He stared in disbelief as the old man piled the
shredded paper onto the table, some of the pieces
falling into the rings of spilt beer.

Ranting and swearing gathered in his throat,
but he could see there was little point. The old
man had fallen into the habit of shredding things,
forming mouse-nest piles which he fumbled or
forgot, depending on his mood.

Jack reached for the papers, hoping he might
retrieve something, but as his fingers touched the

fragments, he felt the papery skin of his father's hand on his.

'You don't want that, son,' he said, for the first time looking into Jack's eyes. 'Never wanted anything to do with Venables – he's always been bad news,' he said, pointing to the shreds. 'Family's what you want – look after your own, I say.'

That's all well and good, Jack wanted to snap, if your family had anything to look after each other with. His father had long since retreated to that childlike place where things should be available for a wistful look or a pocketful of buttons. So the cheque had been the last resort – the only way to unlock the dream Jack had nurtured for years – to have his own company, not to be answering to some anonymous someone a million miles from his own world. He'd smarmed his way through countless calls and late-night drinking sessions to get the ear of Max Venables, the only man who could come up with the goods, realising he was probably selling his soul, but determined to get within touching distance of the star he was desperate to follow. But now, the entirety of his dream was nothing but shreds on a bar-room table.

Jack managed to collect the pieces while his dad was distracted by someone at the bar disagreeing their tab, angling at something for nothing. He stuffed the papers into his pocket, then patiently fought to get his dad into a too-tight anorak, for a fourth then a fifth time talking him through the actions needed to get themselves back to the old man's flat.

He was exhausted by the time he slumped into his own armchair. Hardly bothered with his nightly shot of whisky, despite every inch of him feeling like an exposed tooth, too sensitive to be touched, too angry to be soothed.

Jack awoke next morning still slumped in the chair, back aching, legs protesting at the impossible angles into which they'd been folded for the few hours he'd dozed. For a moment he couldn't fathom why he wasn't within the comfortable folds of his bed, but then the vision of the cheque and his prospects, both in shreds, jumped into his thumping head. He swore, pulling himself upright, reaching for the jacket he'd abandoned on the sofa.

The pieces were surprisingly legible. He went to the table, moving aside newspapers, spreading the fragments out, reaching for Sellotape and scissors. An hour of impatient attempts produced a cheque with most of the details intact.

In the bathroom, Jack splashed water on his face, stared at the mirror to see if yesterday's shirt would do – decided it wouldn't and changed. Making himself as presentable as his bleariness would allow, he drove into town.

'I'm really sorry Mr Jenkins. I do sympathise with what's happened,' the girl in the red suit was saying. 'But we simply can't accept it.' She pointed at the cheque, which, under the bank's fluorescent lighting, looked embarrassingly amateur. 'Perhaps you could speak to the issuer – ask for a duplicate? I'm sure they'd oblige – it's not as if you've cashed this one already, is it?'

But Jack knew there was no way Max Venables would even discuss the matter. You got one chance with him, and there'd be no sympathy for an old man losing his marbles. He must have looked bereft, for the young woman repeated her words. 'I really am sorry Mr Jenkins ...'

And before he could say anything his mobile rang. He was about to cancel the call – couldn't bear to speak to anyone - but saw his father's number. Sighing, he made his way to the door. 'Yes Dad – what's up?'

But it wasn't his father. It was a voice trying hard to be sympathetic, failing. 'Mr Jenkins? I'm afraid I've got ...'

But the bad news was already in Jack's head – as soon as he'd heard the unfamiliar voice on his father's phone. 'It would have been quick' – he heard that much. 'Would you be able to come …'. He heard that too. But he needed to sit down. He slumped onto the bench under the tree, just outside the bakery; watched the passing feet; observed a dog peeing against the café sign. He might have sat for an hour or a minute. A young woman came up, holding his phone. 'I think you dropped this …' she was saying. 'Are you okay? Can I get you something?'

He must have looked hideous, for she continued. 'You're very pale – I could call …?'

'No – I'm okay. Just had a bit of a shock that's all. I'll be alright – you get on.'

'Well, if you're sure …' She took a few paces, looked back, then continued on her way.

It was the nicest anyone had been to him in a lifetime. Several lifetimes he thought, as he dragged himself up and tried to remember where he'd left the car.

Reluctantly he drove to his father's flat, not wanting to see whatever there might be to see, hoping he had already been taken away.

The young policeman had presumably been instructed to stay until the premises could be handed over. Jack thanked him, assuming he'd

61

been the one to call from his father's phone, thinking him too young for that world-weary voice. And closed the door. He was aware of the world going on outside, but the quietness within pressed into his ears. The clock ticking on the mantelshelf. The whirring of the fridge in the tiny kitchen. For want of anything better, Jack began opening cupboards and drawers, noticing the plastic containers of lentils and dried peas which had been there since before his mother had gone; the aged flour bags given away by their outdated prices. The only recent items were packets of budget biscuits. Absentmindedly, Jack opened the fig rolls and fed three, one after another, into his mouth. He hadn't eaten since yesterday. In the drawer to the side of the cooker was a jumble of implements - peelers and ice cream scoops and a plastic rolling pin he remembered his mother filling with ice cubes. 'Ice cold – that's what you need for good pastry Jack.' He picked it up, expecting cheap lightness, but it was heavier than it looked. He shook it. Something inside, sliding solidly.

He took off the end, peered in. It was stuffed with paper. He tugged at the contents, knowing this wasn't important - other things he should be doing. He scrabbled in the drawer, finding a metal skewer. He scooped it round inside the plastic tube and gradually the paper squirmed its way to the entrance; with more encouragement it fell out.

A roll of twenty-pound notes. Then another. He couldn't help himself. He counted them. Five hundred pounds - in each.

Something had started within him. He felt there would be more. He *knew*. He looked around. Where would you put money in this small space? Tins and boxes seemed too obvious. But the Bird's Custard Powder tin looked older even than the lentils and the peas. It yielded another grand. The freezer. He'd heard of all sorts being hidden in freezers. But there was nothing amongst the anaemic sausages and economy ice cream.

There had to be more. The cutlery tray in the sideboard, with the best knives and forks; he lifted it out, finding beneath a life insurance policy. Ridiculously small amounts paid week after week to the Prudential man, but nevertheless …. Jack stuffed it in his pocket. He remembered, as he scanned the overcrowded room, that there'd been something about the dining chairs, something he'd discovered as a child, thinking only he knew. He turned one over, peeled back the lining, revealed more cash. Another chair. Cushions. The tea caddy. The

Quality Street tin with the crinoline lady and the soldier.

An hour, two, had gone by. Jack slumped at the table, over-dosed on biscuit sugar and his findings. He surveyed the haul. Counted roughly in his head. Stopped when he reached the equivalent of the torn cheque, still in his pocket. He hadn't even started on the bedroom yet. Had there been some logic – some small ray of clarity amongst the fog of his father's dwindling mind? Had he actually known what he was doing when he'd ripped up the dubious cheque? 'I hope so.' Jack's smile was creased by his tears as he opened the bedroom door. 'I really bloody hope so.'

TEETERING ON THE EDGE

It had been a difficult year. Agnes Whitehead contemplated while she stirred her eleven o'clock coffee, still having no idea why her reluctance to "be flexible" in her job, to "look at the bigger picture", had turned her world, and her employment status, upside down. Stability, she decided, was what was needed – routine, familiarity – that was what would help her make it through her tribulations.

By lunchtime she had packed, checked, and repacked her case; she had called the station and checked the time of the train and the cost of the ticket. She had emptied her savings tin of fifty pence pieces and counted them into cash bags, ready for the taxi at the other end… as she had done every year.

She had though, been disconcerted when she'd called the hotel. Mrs Appleby, who always took her booking, always confirmed the same room, who wished her 'safe journey my lovely', had not been there. Agnes had spoken to a man - implausibly named Darius. He had joked with her, complimented her voice and efficiency; neither of which was in question as far as Agnes was concerned, and certainly didn't elicit the giggling response which Darius seemed to expect.

He had however, competently taken the details of Agnes' booking; but in response to her demand for her usual room with a view had replied, 'I'll make a note of your preferences Mrs Whitehead, but I can't guarantee we'll be able to fulfil them.'

She wanted to tell him that she wasn't in fact *Mrs* Whitehead, that she didn't want him to 'make a note'; she wanted him simply to do what she was asking, as Mrs Appleby had always done. But her courage abandoned her and she put down the phone, tearing a page from the 'telephone messages' pad which always sat beside it – the page with her 'booking reference number', something which had never been necessary with Mrs Appleby.

Saturday came. The repacked case was at the front door; Agnes had made her fourth tour of the house, rechecking every window, door and electrical switch. She had dithered on her neighbour's offer to 'check things over', which would mean the door being relocked without her supervision. Mr Tadworthy had never been reliable in her eyes, but the Neighbourhood Watch had pointed out that a week's post on the mat was a tell-tale sign of a property ripe for burgling. The keys reluctantly left her fingers; she almost turned to retrieve them, but no, she must do the sensible thing. She did however, cast a glance from the back of the taxi, checking whether the man had already gone inside to trawl through her belongings.

The station was far busier than she had ever seen it, and Agnes wished she had bought ahead, rather than having to queue for her ticket. And then she found that the price quoted on Tuesday was in fact the mid-week special and "should never have been given to her". Today's figure was half as much again, and Agnes had to fiddle at the bottom of her handbag for her 'holiday treats' purse, to make up the difference. The man behind her in a football shirt strained to the point of bursting was swearing none too quietly, and his looming presence at her shoulder flustered Agnes still more.

'No, *madam*…' the ticket clerk's emphasis on the word elevated it to an insult. 'You've given me five tens, instead of five twenties.' She took the money back and searched for more, dropping two notes in the process, and only just managing to retrieve them from beneath the football man's plimsoll.

Well, at least I've allowed myself plenty of time, Agnes thought as she slotted everything back in its rightful place in her bag. She looked around for somewhere she might get her morning coffee, but thought she should first check the departure board. Before she could do so, there was an announcement.

'Network West apologises for the late arrival of the 10.15 train to Bluewater Bay. This is due to leaves on the line, and we are undertaking all necessary actions to resolve the issue. The train is now expected at 12.30. Once again, Network West apologises …'

'Leaves on the line!' Agnes exclaimed to no-one in particular. 'It's June – we don't have leaves on the line in June …'

A young lad next to her muttered.

'I'm sorry?' Agnes enquired.

'Global warming,' he repeated. 'That's what they'll put it down to – it's the excuse for everything these days.'

Agnes checked her watch, the station clock, then her watch again. If the train was two hours late, she would miss the taxi she had booked at the other end, miss afternoon tea in the garden of the Bluewater Hotel, wouldn't have time to unpack before dinner and …

'Network West apologises for the incorrect data report issued at oh nine twenty-five. The 10.15 train to Bluewater Bay will be leaving at 10.40…' Agnes sighed with relief. 'But will be terminating at Hardcastle Central …' there was a hesitation. '…so not in fact proceeding to Bluewater Bay …'

Agnes was hyperventilating. She staggered to the "Freedom Café" on the concourse and dropped onto a sticky plastic chair. A young girl chewing gum asked for her order. 'Is that cappuccino, latte or mocha? Dairy or oat milk? Standard or decaf?'

'JUST A CUP OF COFFEE – MILK, NO SUGAR!' Agnes was as near to swearing as she had ever been. And she never swore – or raised her voice. She wished she had packed her blood pressure monitor.

No-one assisted Agnes with her case, and she was sweaty and exhausted by the time she'd manhandled it into the train's luggage store. She found a seat, luckily next to the window, but soon realised why it had been vacant. Agnes made it her mission not to be judgemental, but here she had to draw the line. The man in the facing seat was alternating between pickled onion crisps, egg sandwiches, a super-size marshmallow and cookie double-choc bar, and cherry cola, and his body was protesting. Endlessly. From every orifice.

Agnes held her cotton lace handkerchief to her mouth, and continued like that until the train pulled into Hardcastle Central; its lavender scent calmed her, but more importantly it allowed her to conceal the snivelling which she was dismayed to find had overwhelmed her.

The taxi journey to Bluewater was surprisingly straightforward, and she'd only had to endure fifteen minutes of commentary on the recent performance of the England Rugby team. But the moment Agnes arrived at the Bluewater Hotel her breathing went into overdrive once more. The beautifully landscaped frontage which she had always admired had become a car park, covered in shingle, with weeds already showing their heads. There were posters at the entrance about "two-for-ones" at the local chips-with-everything emporium, and an "all you can eat" Chinese restaurant on the seafront. Happy hour had also put in an appearance, and Agnes noted that she could have a pitcher of Sex on the Beach or a Fuzzy Navel, if the mood took her. She rubbed the pain in her chest, hoping it wasn't angina, and went to check in.

She was greeted by Darius, a man who continually pushed his overlong fringe away from his face. He reminded Agnes of an equally irritating young man she had seen in a film recently.

'Enchanted, Mrs Whitehead – delighted to meet you at last.' He fussed over her luggage and led the way, enthusing about the tea and coffee-making facilities in her room. No tray of tea in the lounge then, as provided by Mrs Appleby. Agnes's heart sank. No plate of homemade scones and jam…

Her memories were brought to an abrupt halt by Darius announcing that 'due to circumstances beyond our control' they had been unable to allocate her a room overlooking the cliffs. Instead, her case was dumped – there was no other word for it – in a drab little room facing the wretched car park. Agnes was as near to screaming as she had been since she was twelve and prohibited by her father from attending a Beatles concert.

At six o'clock Agnes dressed for dinner. Her emerald-green cocktail dress lifted her spirits, and she took a matching cashmere shawl from her case. She would take her pre-dinner sherry in the garden, as she had always done, and then enjoy her evening meal. She would put the day's disasters behind her and begin her holiday anew.

But, no amontillado – and no sherry glasses either. Agnes had to make do with a small tumbler and Harveys Bristol Cream. Wincing at the sweetness, she asked the waitress if she could still get to the garden via the side door. The girl frowned. 'I'll get Darius,' she muttered, scurrying away.

'Now then Mrs Whitehead, what can we do for you?' He seemed genuinely keen to help, but she wished she could look him in the eye without the curtain of hair hiding his expression. 'Kylie tells me you were wanting the garden, but that's not going to be possible, I'm afraid…'

Before the poor man could finish, something in Agnes snapped. She ranted for a full five minutes about the quality of service she had expected at this establishment, and the standards which seemed to have 'fallen off a cliff' since her last visit. Eventually she came to a full stop, and was deflated to find that Darius was observing her with a mixture of amusement and concern.

'My dear lady,' he started, and continued quickly when Agnes inhaled for another tirade. 'Mrs Whitehead – forgive me. I assumed you knew – that someone had explained... but it seems not,' he said gently. 'I think you'd better come with me.'

And he led Agnes out through the garden until they reached the mid-point. Agnes sighed, as if she had at last returned to her remembered Shangri-la. The apple tree was still there, burgeoning with early fruit, and flowerbeds still overflowed with peonies and hydrangeas. She stepped forward, keen to take in the sunset over the sea. But Darius grabbed her arm. 'Mrs Whitehead – I'm sorry, but you can go no further.' He held her elbow and together they crept just two tentative steps.

There beneath her, the remaining garden of the Bluewater Hotel had taken a nose-dive into the sea. Even as they stood, there was the rattle of falling shale and a sod of grass slipped to its demise. Agnes stretched her neck, catching just a glimpse of the rocks, clay and stone now flowing like a waterfall down to the beach. Her beloved Bluewater. Even this was abandoning her. She gulped but still a strangled cry escaped as her legs buckled. Nothing – but nothing – stayed the same; even nature was against her. She sobbed, allowing Darius to help her stand.

He held fast to her arm, ushering her back to the hell which was Happy Hour. Agnes didn't once look up from her sherry, refusing to acknowledge the skimpy outfits and the raucous laughter that accompanied the cocktail pitchers.

Later she would return to the garden, she decided, when they were all preoccupied with their two-for-ones and their buckets of drink; and she would make her way to the end of the crumbling lawn, sit on the edge and allow herself to slide down with the rocks, and join the only familiar thing left to her - the sea.

TOMORROW AND TOMORROW AND TOMORROW

– a diary of time

<u>Wednesday 9th November</u>

We're wasting too much time – it's official. Not just you and me – oh no – Fiona Bruce has just announced on the 6 o'clock news that 'as a nation and as a planet, we are using up the commodity of time at an unprecedented rate.' Apparently, the cabinet is meeting as we speak; announcements are imminent.

<u>Thursday 10th November</u>

We've just had one of those 'doom and gloom' speeches from the PM – where he looks earnestly into the camera and tells us we've all been very bad and that we need to take 'the severest actions' to put right the error of our ways. Oh Joy. They currently have working parties scrutinising the areas where the most wastage is taking place, and recommendations will follow. They have already pointed the finger though at media in all its formats – well, in its electronic forms anyway.

Friday 11th November

Rationing. Would you believe it, they are bringing in rationing – from midnight tonight we are all restricted to using Twitter, Facebook, TikTok and any other electronic gobblers-up of time to just TWO hours a day. And there may be further cuts if that doesn't bring about the gains in time needed. Television is also severely restricted – unless of course you are watching David Attenborough or Lucy Worsley, or anything else which can vaguely be classed as educational.

Ps Apparently, Google has also managed to slip in under the banner of 'educational', as that is the only place where children might find the answers to their homework, and adults the solutions to The Times crossword and any number of bar-room arguments. Using it to check the opening times for Primark, or the price of cider at Wetherspoons, is of course, not permitted.

Monday 14th November

No further announcements over the weekend, but there have been animated demonstrations across the country about the social media rationing. The PM has apparently said that at least protesting is getting people out in the fresh air and away from their devices – which in itself is a better use of time, and therefore achieving his objectives.

Tuesday 15th November

I've been looking at my own lifestyle (as requested by said PM) and have come up with quite a list of time-wasters …

1. Being asked to complete customer satisfaction surveys when all I've done is to enquire about a shop's opening hours.

2. Trying to remember the answer to 'which security question would you like to give the answer to?' How am I supposed to know the answer when I can't even remember the question?

3. Queuing – why wasn't that at the top of my list? The Post Office in particular should be brought before the High Court to explain why they are taking such liberties with the public's time.

4. And, and – and I can't even type quickly enough to get this one down – phone queuing! My blood pressure is rising at the very thought of the amount of time I have literally allowed to flow down the drain, listening to teeth-grinding music and a woman assuring me that my call is important to her.

Coincidentally, and rather spookily, the Government has just announced that companies and corporations will be charged additional taxes (windbag as opposed to windfall) for encouraging the country to waste inordinate amounts of time sitting in call queues. Maybe this whole "time crisis" has some merits after all.

Wednesday 16th November

Or maybe not. Today the PM has done another of his public broadcasts, telling us that, as well as rationing, there will be a need to "recycle" our time. The details, as ever, will be released over the next few days. I'm just trying to think how that might work. Am I going to be expected to collect up Bert Holloway's filthy bits of time that he wastes ogling young mothers in the park, or Elsie Taverner's bingo sessions? Bingo – now there's a subject that splits the nation even more than Brexit – waste of time or enriching, entertaining social experience? Good luck with sorting that one out PM.

And anyway, what will I do when I find these spare bits of time? Will there be a scheme for knitting them into nice new blankets of time that can be donated to the time-poor? Will they provide us all with time-composters where we can stuff in the garbage spouted by politicians and get good quality conversations coming out at the bottom?

And talking of garbage, I'm just about to fire off another e-mail to the Home Secretary – about sports commentators, and football pundits in particular. There must be container-loads of wasted time in all that tosh they spout … for hours and hours and hours, before the game, after the game, during the game. They alone could retrieve the time-deficit and get the country's books back in balance without any further measures. Come on – step up to the plate Gary Lineker.

Thursday 24th November

No reply from the Home Sec. I think she's leaving it long enough that she will be able to announce the idea as her own and collect an instant damehood.

Friday 25th November

Well, it appears that time is not so much going to be recycled as "re-enacted". I think they must have seen the difficulties of us all using each other's wasted time, but what they have come up with as an alternative is – to use the government's phrase-of-the-moment – eyewatering.

We are to be given the opportunity to live again some of our favourite days. Suggestions have to be submitted by the end of the day, and there will then be a referendum – 'Time For The Nation To Speak', it's being dubbed.

Tuesday 29th November

The votes are in, and predictably our best days are – Super Saturday at the 2012 Olympics, any/all of the Queen's jubilees, and the 1966 World Cup. What a strange nation we are.

Saturday 17th December

It seems that we have re-used our favourite days so much that they are rapidly wearing thin. They now need to be preserved as "national treasures" and have been decamped to the V&A for restoration and conservation. So much for recycling, but another announcement is coming soon …

Wednesday 21st December

Despite all efforts, the supply of time is running critically low and urgent action is needed. TOP27 (UN Time Change Conference of the Parties) has agreed that all nations will – from today – not be allowed to waste any further new days. We will all stay in this day – Wednesday 21st December - for the foreseeable future.

I am stunned into wordlessness.

Wednesday 21st December

We are now watching repeats of repeats of repeats of Dad's Army - and The Sound of Music, The Great Escape and The Wizard of Oz are on constant replay. The recurring news has become so monotonous that it has been declared a waste of time in its own right and banished to the recycling centre. Ditto the PM.

Wednesday 21st December

Hurray! Julie Andrews was interrupted in the middle of her Favourite Things for us to be told that the Government is making a U-turn. They haven't of course called it that – it is a 'Re-evaluation of the Unfolding Crisis', but who cares. They have realised that bringing time to a standstill in the middle of winter, when the days are at their shortest, has reduced the opportunities for people to save time, because "there is less usable time available". Is that what is known as a paradox? Never mind. It means that at midnight there will be – taddahh!! – a new tomorrow!

Wednesday 21st December

Apparently not. While every world government has been prevaricating, time itself has run out - literally. It would appear that there has been an imperceptible but significant leak in Hershey, Pennsylvania and another in Cooper Pedy, Australia, neither of which anyone had picked up on. Time has simply been escaping, ebbing constantly into the universe. So, while we were all striving to save an hour here, a second there – making the best possible use of our own inconsequential portions of time, and using up other people's leftovers - precious minutes were simply draining away.

So, I've taken myself up onto the moors, with two bottles of my best Malbec, and I'm sitting here under the dark sequinned skies, waiting for all the time in the world to finally seep away. As a shooting star hurtles past, I raise a glass to it, realising as I do so that it is taking with it the last seconds of tomorrow. I wait for something significant to mark the occasion – a bang, or a whimper; but Mr Shakespeare had it right after all – the rest is silence.

MEMOIR OF A LOST GRANDMOTHER

This story is based on the few things I have been told about my paternal grandmother, who died when I was only a few months old. I have her autograph book in my possession and have tried to weave the contents of that book, together with stories told by my father, into a "memoir" that she might have written

I had been looking for photographs of my son, Eric, wanting to show his wife the similarities between him as a baby and his daughters – the same dark eyes and gentle curls. But as I rooted around in the drawer filled with seaside postcards and fountain pens, my fingers fell on the leather-bound book. Just holding it in my hand made me smile, and I couldn't help but untie the ribbons and let it fall open. The colours were still bright on the little painting of a barrow overflowing with pansies which filled one of the pages.

The book had been given to me by my older sister, Dollie, and friends and relatives had begun to fill the pages with their rhymes and sayings. Kenyon though had gone a step further, and had added a little watercolour painting each time he visited. He had a real skill, and all my sisters teased that he must have a crush, to spend so much time painting these beautiful little pictures for me.

As I look at his work, it takes me back to the front parlour of my parents' house. I can see us all sitting there - my sister Jennie and Kenyon and his friend. This book is open on the table in front of us, and beside it a miniature paint box and two fine brushes in a jam-jar of water. We are all chattering, one word on top of another, until the back door slams in the breeze, and Kenyon looks up. He gathers his brushes and paints. 'I'd better go,' he says, and is out of the front door before father appears in his overalls, grime streaked across his brow.

'You girls okay?' he says, but his face darkens as he spots the painting, not yet dry, on the table. He says nothing, but I know that I'm already blushing.

Because you see, Dad too was aware of Kenyon being "sweet" on me, but I was only seventeen and it was all too much for him. He was afraid that Kenyon would whisk me away from him, and worse still would later abandon me, and he couldn't bear to see anything bad happen to any of "his girls". 'You're not to see him any more,' Dad had said firmly. It didn't last, I could always twist Dad round my little finger, but the dejection was always there in his eyes after that, as if he could never rid himself of the idea that Kenyon might hurt his little girl.

Once Dad has gone to scrub himself at the kitchen sink, I look back through the pages of the book, at the collection of pictures which Kenyon has created. Each time he hands me one of these little gifts, our affection for each other grows. 'We'll go and live at the seaside,' he would say; 'I'll paint pictures for the trippers and we'll get rich, and I'll buy you crab for tea.'

But Dad's disapproval was too much in the end. I couldn't bear to see him upset, and Kenyon couldn't see me distressed, and our friendship wilted, unlike the flowers he'd painted.

I carry on turning the pages of the book, and there is middle-sister Millie's firm bold handwriting. I remember her nagging me for weeks on end, when, after George and I had married, we made the decision to move to Waterend. It was George's decision really, his work was taking him to Hemel Hempstead and he'd found this lovely little cottage in the nearby village. But Millie, a true London girl, thought it would be the end of the world. 'You'll be an outsider there, you know - they won't talk to you, Maggie dear. And there'll be no running water – all those country yokels do their washing in the river – you'll be up to your armpits in pondweed.'

She'd been right, about the running water at least – we'd had to use the pump in the yard, creaking like old bones as it strained to pull the water from deep underground. At night I'd often stand at the cottage door. I'd been so used to the streetlamps back in Kentish Town but here I could see nothing, not even a shadow. That blackness, with nothing to disturb it but an owl, had frightened me at first, but then I'd found the compensation of the stars; I never remembered really seeing them in London, but here there were so many, fighting each other for space in the sky. And Millie couldn't have been more wrong about the locals.

On our first day Mr Blackstock had brought eggs. 'You'll be hungry with all that fetching and carrying', he'd said, and there was a basket of raspberries for Eric. Over the weeks, Mrs B would call in on her way to collect firewood after a storm, or to harvest the hedgerows for jam. Eric would end up plastered with purple blackberry juice, as he carried one to my basket and put three in his mouth. Early on Sunday morning I'd lie in bed, listening to the rain clattering onto the tiled roof, or the woodpigeon calling from the tall tree, and I'd feel comfortable and content curled up in my eiderdown.

One Tuesday, when I was walking in the lane, a woman called to me from her cottage garden. It was a bigger house than ours, and I was trying to take it all in as I followed her up the path.

'I've seen you a few times.' Her permed curls and lipstick were so stylish – far too glamorous for Waterend – and I was overawed by her, but when she spoke, she was just an ordinary London girl like me.

She made tea, and brought out fancy chocolate biscuits, and made us both laugh as she described her shortcomings as a housewife.

'I could help if you like,' I said, without even thinking about it, knowing I could easily make a difference to the dusty rooms. Later, when I told George, he teased me about mixing with the rich and famous.

'What do you mean?' I asked.

'Well, that's John Tilley's wife – you know, him from the wireless. They met at the Windmill Theatre.'

But the fame meant nothing to me. She was a friend and our two families became friends. Kate had no children, so she took young Eric to Whipsnade Zoo when it first opened; although she'd complained like anything about her aching feet after a day walking in stilettos. But the best time was when she traded her gramophone with us for a cage of George's prize canaries. We couldn't believe our luck, to have this wonderful thing which, with a few winds of the handle, would play music for us. From time to time George would bring home a precious gramophone record from a shop in Hemel Hempstead, balanced carefully on the back of his motorbike, and after dinner we would dance and dance late into the night.

Sister Dolly was seven years older than me, which had seemed like a lifetime when I was ten, but as the years passed we became best friends. It was Dolly who had explained the whole thing to me about Dad and Kenyon. I hadn't realised until then that Dad had left his family in Coventry when he was not much more than a boy, following the work on the railways to Cambridge and then London, so that, unlike his family, he would always have money in his pocket. I remember the oily blackness ingrained into the creases of his hands, and that smell of oil which never left his clothes – he never seemed to stop working, and all so that "my girls" as he called us all, would have a better life than him.

Dolly had given me the autograph book as a sort of leaving present. I'd been distraught when she'd told me she was marrying for a second time. I'd got so used to having her at home again that I didn't want her to leave, but I knew that she needed to make a new life for herself and her baby, Frances and when Harold came along she had to take the opportunity which offered itself. Her first husband had died in the last days of the Great War, and I shudder to think what the poor man experienced in the trenches, only to be declared dead on arrival at Dover.

We still got on well over the next few years, and I was of course happy to share my new life with Dolly when it finally arrived. I used to have Dolly's children to stay at Waterend from their home in Hendon, so that they could run in the fields and fish in the river; Frances, by that time a young woman herself, would cycle with me round the narrow lanes. It made Eric laugh, whenever I told the story of going to Ashridge with her and getting locked inside the Bridgewater Monument, because some lads had told the gatekeeper that no-one was left at the top, and he had locked the door and gone for tea.

A paper flutters out of the autograph book – 'Banque de France, Dix Francs' – a souvenir from Eric when he came home on leave. George had been nearly forty when the second world war started, and although I wasn't religious, I prayed that he'd stay in England, away from active service when he joined the RAF in 1940. Thankfully, he was posted to Yorkshire, and although that meant long train journeys, standing all the way to see him for just a few hours, at least he was safe, and I could keep in touch. Eric was another matter. He was just a young man and I knew that he would probably be sent into the thick of it. He volunteered for the RAF too, but they wouldn't take him as anything other than a Rear Gunner – which everyone knew was an immediate death sentence. At least that meant he was with me for a while longer, while he awaited his call-up papers. He finally received them in 1942, and it wasn't until he walked off to the station that I realised it would be the first time I'd ever lived on my own. I was so used to having my sisters and then George around – but I managed the emptiness by pretending that George and Eric had just gone on a jaunt like they used to - out for hours on the river, in a rickety rowing boat. This time, I convinced myself they'd gone for a few days, to the seaside perhaps, and they'd be back with a jug or an ashtray, with "made in Brighton" painted across its face.

It was ironic, though, that their leaving opened the door for me to do the one thing I'd always longed to do. As a girl I'd wanted to be a nurse, but instead I'd gone to work in the biscuit factory, tearing my fingers to shreds packing gritty Nice biscuits; then I moved to work in a shop – because those were the jobs you did when you left school at thirteen. The war allowed me to resurrect my dream, and I trained with the Red Cross, tending the victims of bomb blasts and fires. I thought constantly of Eric as I helped the injured, but at the same time I was guiltily envious of him and his fellow soldiers, seeing parts of the world I would only ever see at the pictures – the Pyramids and the Sphinx, the sacred rivers of India. The furthest I ever travelled was Yorkshire, and even now a bit of me wishes I could have followed in their travelling footsteps.

I keep turning the pages until finally there is George. His entry is in beautiful curled copperplate lettering, with his signature upside down in the corner – telling you all there is to know about George. We met when I started work at the International Stores in Hendon, and he charmed me from the start with his stories and his conjuring tricks. We started walking out, but it had to be a huge secret; if the shop manager found out I would have had to leave – there was no fraternising between trainee managers and shop girls in those days. George ignored me at work, pretending he didn't even like me, but his zest for life was impressed on everything he did.

It had been George who'd been delighted when I fell pregnant with Eric, and George who dealt with father's disappointment at our hasty marriage. On our wedding day he was splendid in his winged shirt collar and bow tie, and he gave me this beautiful mother-of-pearl watch. I had nothing to give him, but he wiped away my tears, saying that I was a gift in myself, and that Eric was the icing on the cake.

'Are you okay up there, Mrs P?'

My daughter-in-law is calling, and I slip the book back into the drawer. I'll leave it there for the two little girls downstairs to find, when they're old enough to understand.

THE GIFT

This story won the Wyvern Prize in the 2019 Wells Literary Festival competition

He had tried – a hundred times it seemed – to get her what she wanted. He didn't understand of course, why would he? – but Emrys had heard of such things before, whispered in the corners of the snug or muttered at the kitchen table, wrapped up with the potato peelings. He'd taken his worries to his mother, while she was lathering the shirt collars, so that he didn't have to look her in the eye. 'It's nothing unusual,' she'd told him, 'Women in her condition often have their "cravings"'.

The word had fascinated him – Emrys had never come across "cravings" before, and it had an insistency about it, an urgency that was not to be ignored. He found himself saying it over and over as he unravelled his nets and re-knotted the holes, and thinking back he was sure now that it was that word which had started off this other sensation which over the days had begun to fill his head.

No matter what he was doing, where he was going, he found that once the thing had started, he couldn't stop himself. And it manifested itself particularly when he was here – sitting on his small boat, on the oil-calm waters, trying to do his best for Bethan. As he gazed at the morning sky, fresh and not yet ogled or dirtied by the myriad of people who would move beneath it over the course of the day, the words just tumbled into his head. He had no idea where they came from – words he didn't even know he knew – like 'opulent' or 'elixir' or 'onomatopoeia'. But there they were, effervescing like an ale that had been poured too quickly, gushing over the edge of his being. He didn't know what to do with them – they slipped through his fingers most of the time, like rippling mackerel, silvery and quick, but occasionally one would stay with him – like 'mellifluous' or 'lilting'. But there were so many of them, and they were so beautiful, that eventually he knew that he had to save them somehow. Ignoring his nets which were wafting on the tide he searched the boat and then his pockets and eventually found a stub of pencil and a shrivelled scrap of paper – big enough to squeeze on twenty words. He managed thirty, but as he looked up from his work he realised he had drifted along the coast and that his nets were still empty. Bethan would be distraught but he couldn't help himself. Even as he managed to scoop up an errant few dabs as he neared the shore, he was still gathering the words.

Before he took his fishing boat out on Tuesday Emrys knew he needed to make sure that he was better equipped. He stood in the shadows of the chandler's shop and when the pavement outside the small post office was empty, he sneaked in and purchased a small notepad – with its cobalt sheets of Basildon Bond - pretending it was for his mother. He found a decent pencil in the sideboard drawer and stowed them both deep inside his overall pockets.

That morning the sewin, those wonderful Welsh sea trout, were still not playing and he had no idea how he was going to return to Bethan empty-handed once more, with not a single trout to put in front of her. Over the weeks he had brought her cod and hake and herring, but nothing else would do – she wanted sewin, and if he couldn't bring her that, then really what was the point of him being married to her, she had screamed at him again last night.

This slight to his manhood – as Emrys saw it – cut him to the quick. He was determined to put aside the words and divert all his efforts into his fishing and prove her wrong - but then he'd had to run to Mary Evan's shelves at the library to satisfy himself about the word "quick" - and the fact that it could mean "alive" as well as "fast" was a revelation to him, and he had had to add it to his notebook before it slipped out of his head.

And so even the worry of Bethan and the elusive fish … and there was another one of those words, he thought, as he pulled his notebook from inside his pocket – even that worry was already slithering away from him, overtaken by a new catch of words, waiting to be heaved in and harvested, as he headed once more to sea.

The pencil scribbled faster and faster, recording the words at horizontals and diagonals and crosshatchings around the page as they overtook him, until at last he was sated, and slumped back on his seat. He tilted his head, allowing the rising sun to warm his face, but as he glanced down he noticed that it had tinted the paper rose and lilac, and that beneath the shaft of colourful light the words seemed to be forming themselves into some sort of order, like soldiers falling into line. Emrys blinked in the sun's intensity, baffled and bewildered. A poem had somehow formed itself, there in front of him – and he, Emrys, had obviously written it!

Immediately he hauled his cumbersome nets onto the deck and set the boat back towards the harbour. The order he had promised the Crown and Anchor for their lunchtime trippers was forgotten; so was the fishy seaweed odour wafting from his jersey as he ran clumsily in his gumboots down the lane to the cottage he was in danger of no longer sharing with Bethan. His creation was imbued with "opulence", he thought, "positively quivering" with love and romance, the "very essence of generosity". Bethan might have a craving for sewin, but even she must see that this offering of his, this work to rival anything the best Eisteddfod might ever have seen, was far superior to any sea trout. But as he ran with the paper in his hands, Bethan appeared at the doorway, frying pan in hand, and every word he had ever discovered suddenly slipped from his skin like scales; every word that is except "catastrophe".

OPEN WINDOW

Church bells pealing. Stirring the already hot air. Only 10.30, but already Mediterranean, and that is why I sit, not in the parched garden, but at the window. Just outside, a bee has been caught in a newly formed cobweb, and its wriggling to be free catches the attention of a sparrow. The bird flits, trying from every angle to access this unexpected meal, but to no avail.

Inside, the room is cool – thick solid Victorian walls having no truck with the outside temperatures – and a gentle breeze is wafting the curtains, giving the illusion of a more normal day.

For as well as the heat, today is *not* normal – not in any way, general or particular. I continue to listen to the bells, imagining myself to be there, at the top of the hill, chattering to those I haven't seen in years, adjusting my hat as it's lifted by the breeze, allowing the chimes to raise my spirits. But this is as near as I will be.

I have attended enough weddings to have the gist of the service in my head, and I take myself through it, finding myself a pew, nodding to a distant cousin, turning at the sound of the wedding march, smiling at the exuberant happiness of the girl walking up the aisle. A hymn – what would it be? I myself would have chosen "I vow to thee my country" – if they would have allowed me to change the words. I've always thought "I vow to thee forever" would be so much more appropriate for so many occasions ... but the music itself is precious because it is "Jupiter" from the Planet Suite, - the bringer of joy, and the ruling planet of my birth sign - and so I have always claimed it as my own.

And then the words – the vows. "To have and to hold, from this day forward ...for better for worse ... so long as ye both shall live." To have been able to have anything - or anyone - for as long as I have lived would have been a precious gift indeed, but it was not to be, and my joys have always had to be sought elsewhere.

I watch as the regular gang of sparrows lords it around the garden, relishing the absence of people, taking the opportunity to fly low, skimming the tops of the salvias and roses, dive-bombing the wilting marigolds to find their way down into the dust bowl they have created beneath the shrubs, then off again to chatter like girls, in the bird bath, as they splash arcs of rainbow droplets into the air.

I wonder, if I stand on tiptoe, whether I can see as far as the church? I can spot it easily at night, lit up and standing proudly at the top of the hill, but in the harsh sunlight it blends with the procession of houses marching up to meet it. I have a thought, and shuffle my arthritic way to the bottom of the staircase, dragging on the banister as I attempt to meet the challenge of the steps that I haven't battled with for many a year.

In the time it takes, I think that the wedding party, the white dress and the flowers, and the young girls with baskets of petals, will have arrived and moved into the coolness of the church – quickly if they have any sense, but the joy of the day and the desire not to miss a moment of it will make them oblivious to any problem.

Oblivious to me too.

I have forgotten about all my belongings – my temptation to send everything 'upstairs' over the years – out of sight is out of mind – and I have to manoeuvre around lampshades and crates of books, a sewing machine and a basket of fabrics; an electric fan, covered in cobwebs, which would be useful today, but it will be hard enough to get myself back downstairs. I get to the window with a graze on my leg to show for my efforts, and there is my view. A black car, more funereal than marital, and emerging from it a froth of white. She looks beautiful, even though I can't make out her face. And girls in pink are fluttering around her like moths, and a man I don't recognise is offering his arm to her, guiding her towards the church door. I clear a space on a rickety chair – moving curtains I don't remember seeing in any room, and a crocheted blanket, blues and greens which remind me of the sea, and which I think I will take back down with me. I sit on the precarious seat – propped more than seated – and wait for the second act to begin, and the cast to re-appear.

The bells begin again, and there is a rush, an exuberance of froth and flowers and showers of confetti. And then, there he is. The boy I have seen, here and there, for years – a tot, a schoolboy, a student and now a husband. The boy who looked handsome and lively, but who never waved, because he never knew who I was; who scooted past or cycled, or walked with friends past my door as I tried to keep track, to observe without being observed.

And now here he is, the man laughing in the sunshine and the showers of bells, and I raise my hand to acknowledge him, though he's unable to sec me.

Here he is – the boy I gave away.

SALAD DAYS

'That boy! He's as green as a gooseberry!'

Magda looks up from the phone she has been staring at for more than ten minutes while the toddler in her charge is throwing cereal across the floor.

'Goose – berry? What is this "goose-berry"?'

Caroline and Giles glance over at her as if they had forgotten her existence. They have been so totally absorbed in their character assassination of their best friends' son that they have been oblivious to Magda's tap-tapping of messages with her fuchsia-painted nails, or of their young child who, it seems, is intent on re-decorating their garden-room kitchen with Ready Brek.

For a moment, the three are caught in a staring triangle, each with eyebrow raised, silently questioning what the other might be talking about, until Magda breaks the spell.

'Goose-berry,' she repeats with an exaggerated slowness, allowing the words to pout her well-glossed lips. 'I have met 'goose' – yes, goose is good, Christmas dinner – delish,' she says, mimicking Caroline's current "go-to" word for anything or anyone of which she approves. 'And berry – I know too berry … black-berry, rasp-berry, jelly-belly …'

'Baby, Magda – it's jelly *baby*,' Caroline corrects, smiling tolerantly, mentally storing the vagaries of their latest au pair's grasp of the English language to relate at her next book group meeting.

'Yes, yes, whatever, whatever – but 'goose-berry', tell me about this – this – chicken fruit …'

The child's spoon clangs against the Neff oven, distributing in its wake the last of the glutinous cereal across the immaculate hob.

The couple watch open mouthed, as Magda appears to rescue the spoon, wipe the hob, the baby's face and the floor in one seamless action, whilst at the same time retrieving a selection of wholemeal and seeded toast from the toaster and putting the filled basket on the table in front of them.

They simultaneously close their mouths as Magda pushes plates, locally-sourced honey and refreshed coffee cups towards them.

'So ...' the au pair begins again. 'The chicken berry ...'

'Oh Magda – it's nothing to do with chickens – or geese for that matter,' Caroline laughs, condescension glazing her words. 'It's a fruit, a green fruit like ...' She searches around for a suitable comparison. 'Well, like little tiny plums, really, but hairier.' She sees another barrage of questions forming on Magda's lips as the au pair appears to contemplate the bizarreness of a nation who might consume bearded fruits; she hastens on. 'But we weren't really talking about fruit, were we dear? It's a figure of speech ...' Caroline stops, realising from the expression on Magda's face, that this time she has gone too far off-piste. 'No – it's a ... oh, come on Giles – what is it?' she says, snapping her fingers in exasperation.

'A 'simile', my dear ...' but he too gives up as he sees Magda's shoulders and hands form a questioning shrug. 'Look – forget the grammatical designations – we were just describing our friends' son. He's ...'

'Yes, him who is green. He is sick?' Magda demands to know.

'No, no – no. It's an expression – you know – like "he went as red as a tomato" or "he's as cool as a cucumber".'

'He's a – a – salad?'

'No. No, no.'

Caroline and Giles look at each other, exasperated and exhausted before their working days have even begun; wondering whether the initial appeal of Magda's eccentricity is really worth all this effort.

'Look, Magda – green – it means – you know, naïve, innocent, wet behind the ears …'

'He is always washing his ears, this boy?'

'It's like this Magda,' starts Caroline once more, determined to try a new track to bring this conversation to a conclusion. 'Our friends' son – the boy we're talking about …'

'Who is green, yes …'

'Yes – no,' butts in Giles. 'He's only seventeen – but he thinks he knows what life is all about. And apparently he let slip to his parents the other day that he's been trying to date this older woman …'

'And what colour is she? You see, mixed relationships, they really do not work; black and yellow, pink and green – they are, how do you say – a disaarster waiting to explode – I think.'

'Happen,' Giles corrects, 'A disaster waiting to …'

'Anyway,' Caroline interjects, before they are all side-tracked yet again. 'Anyway …'

'Yes anyway,' Giles takes over, assuming that, with his legal training and talent for public speaking, it really should be his role to tell the story. 'Young Ben thinks he knows everything there is to know about women; he thinks he can seduce this one with a barrage of compliments and flattery - and a few little gifts!'

Caroline looks down into the monotonous greyness of her work suit. A compliment or two doesn't seem such a bad idea to her.

'Yes. Apparently, he spent his entire month's allowance on some silly little necklace for this woman,' Giles carries on, smirking at the ridiculousness of such folly, the misguided optimism of youth.

'And he can't?' asks Magda, playing with something at her neck, absentmindedly rubbing the baby's toast between her fingers. The child begins to howl as he sees his soldiers disappearing into a heap of wholemeal crumbs.

'Well obviously not, no. Totally inappropriate,' says Giles, getting into his stride. 'From what we hear, this woman is worldly wise, beautiful, elegant ... everything, in fact, that poor Ben is not.'

Caroline buries her look further into the pleats of her skirt, but Magda glances up as she takes in Giles' words; flutters her lashes, runs her fingers through her luxuriant red hair. She smiles at herself in the distorted reflexion of the spoon she has retrieved from the floor.

In the silence, Caroline and Giles look up, observing the actions of their au pair. Once more they open their mouths to speak, but no words emerge.

'Oh please – tell me some more,' says Magda, as she realises they are watching her. 'I am – how do you say … intreeeg-ed by your story of this charming young man; all eyes as they say.'

'But that's just it, Magda – don't you see? He's not a man, he's just a boy; he knows nothing of the world, of the complexities of love.' Giles preens, puffing himself up like a cock pheasant. 'Life is simple for him …he just sees the fun and enjoyment, and the kudos of dating an older woman.'

Caroline has a faraway look in her eyes, as if she is yearning for some of that simplicity and fun for herself, for a life far away from three o'clock work deadlines and Giles' endless supper parties and accounts needing to be produced for the Townswomens' Guild. She twists her wedding band on her finger distractedly.

'Oh yes,' says Giles, catching his thumbs in his waistcoat pockets as though he is holding forth at Number 1 court at the Old Bailey, instead of due at the Magistrates at 9.30 for Wayne Ramsbottom's fourteenth appearance. 'Poor old Ben – he's in his salad days … we were all there once …'

'So – I was right all along – he *is* salad.' Magda is indignant. 'You are hiding back truths from me,' she says as she swings the baby from the high chair and clip clops indignantly across the faux granite floor in her high-heeled silver mules. 'It is not right, Mr Dib-er-ley, she says, drawing out the syllables of his name. 'You should have told me before – that this boy is salad, that he is green …' She swings open the hallway door and lets it slam against the imitation marble worktop, causing Giles to wince. 'I *told* you – mixed relationships – they will not work.' She stands in the doorway, hand on hip, but her voice now is little more than a whisper. 'Please do not worry – I will contact poor Benjamin; I may not return his gifts though,' she says, fingering the pretty chain around her neck. 'But I will – as you say – let him go gently.'

And with that Magda is gone, and the couple are left with their cold toast. There is, once more, a silence hanging heavily between them, until Giles returns to safer ground, bemoaning the stresses of the world of law and delinquents who ought to know better. His phone rings out an alarm and he checks it with an exaggerated intake of breath. 'Places to go, people to see,' he says, 'When the going gets tough, as they say …'. He gets to the door before returning and kissing the air at the side of Caroline's cheek. She, on the other hand, remains alone, oblivious to the chaos of her soulless kitchen, allowing the memory of her husband's words to drift around in her head. She distractedly fingers the delicate silver bracelet sitting on her own suntanned wrist, the one which has gone unnoticed by her husband, wondering now if it *she* who's the one who is "salad" – the one who has been green enough to think she was the only woman in Ben Worthington's life.

ESCAPE TO REALITY

There is a noise, and even you are spooked. Not part of your presentation, but something which rouses everyone's speculation.

You look up into the struts and lights of the above-stage world. Wondering if a bird that should be appearing from a hat has decided to make a squawking break for it – possibly taking a white rabbit in its claws.

Until that moment you have been posturing like a Victorian automaton; exchanging a Jack of Clubs for a rose, a borrowed necklace for a coin, with barely a thought moving between your head and your hand. Your fingers draw the audience in, distracting them from the real and into a world of mayhap and possibility. But your thoughts are divorced from the three-card trick, searching as they are for another life to pull out of your hat, a new beginning in the folds of your cloak.

And then you notice it. At the stage-side a spirit dog howls at your fakery, and someone lets it loose.

It bounds toward you, and you side-step - not wanting to tread on something which maybe isn't there, but too much there to risk a biting reaction. Your audience think you are playing the fool, stepping over the invisible, distracting them from the main event. But the main event has left the building – you have lost every inch of concentration and are a bystander too. But only so many empty stage minutes are acceptable, and the pitch of the audience's murmuring is rising. You hightail it, snatching up your box of tricks as you go.

A woman with a bird's head umbrella and a squashed prune of a hat reels toward you - possibly the mistress of the dog - and you raise a forbidding hand. She ignores it and you, ploughing forth, umbrella point prone. You mentally catalogue the items in your box which might fend off this marauding female. Her eye catches yours and you consider the hexes which must be hidden in her voluminous bag – because your control is ebbing, your legs unable to make an escape.

She sweeps you along like a pile of dust, and you find yourself backstage. 'You must help me,' she rasps. The wrong-footing of her words steals your voice; she thrusts her face into yours. 'You MUST help me,' she screeches.

'With what?' is the best you can muster.

'With everything,' she says unhelpfully, shushing you out of the stage door and onto the street. Pigeons find you suddenly attractive, until a show of her umbrella makes them think twice. They whoosh elsewhere, contributing to the dissenting soundtrack of the traffic, as she conjures with the next possible move.

You find yourself in an alleyway, reeking of cabbage carcasses and spilt beer and desperate men. You lift your face in a quest for clean air, but she drags you further into the gloom and detritus. 'I have to recover my daughter,' she says, holding a wretched hand to her chest. You sniff uncertainly at her choice of words, questioning her sanity.

'I'm not a book to be judged,' she snaps. 'Melissa has been gone these past twenty months ... and never re-emerged.' And you sigh at the prospect of a task impossible before it even begins.

'I'm not a magician,' you are about to say, but the box of tricks under your arm reminds you that you are indeed that very thing. 'I'm not a *psychic*,' you try instead.

'Jiggery pokery,' she dismisses. 'Hocus pocus is *not* what is required.' She prods each word into your chest and you wonder what *is* required – what you might actually provide. Suddenly you recall your audience and move to return, to finish what you had started. But the umbrella and the withering look block your way once more.

'Melissa,' she repeats, and you find yourself scanning the windows of the relentless buildings around you, searching for an answer, or the spirit of magicians past who might lift you from this impossibility. No-one shows. 'Where … *how*?' you enquire reluctantly.

'Caught up in a magic trick.' She answers with the assumption that you will shortly be tuned to her wavelength.

You cannot stop yourself asking. '… And which trick …?'

But you know, before she forms a word on her insipid lips, what she is going to say. You know that this will take you back to an end of a pier, at an end-of-the-world shabby seaside resort, where you had persuaded a volunteer from a meagre audience, and hesitated when you had seen it was not the usual brash young female with smiles and skirts and a desire for mischief, but a faded, second-hand sort of woman. Yet to her credit, still with a wish for adventure playing in her grey eyes.

You had taken her hand, escorting her along aisles and up steps, and there she was, more plain still in the glare of the limelight. But she was all you had, and to reject her would be to pack away your magic box, and head for obscurity. So you fussed over her, like a lost dog suddenly home, complimenting, flattering. To give her due, she played along, like a tinselled showgirl, bowing and parading before her audience. You admired her mettle, and, buoyed up, showed off the cabinet into which she would step – back, front, this side, that. She winked, and you wondered whether, for once, it might be you who disappeared. And the thought fleetingly appealed to you – to become 'whereabouts unknown', with speculations abounding that the tail-end of you might have been spotted in a mirror somewhere. But the woman cleared her throat, bringing you back to the present, and you helped her into the box. She waved merrily to the audience before you closed the door. And with a spin of the box and a roll on the drums, she was gone.

But when she should have been back in her audience seat, grinning and accepting her rightful applause, she was not there. Neither was she backstage, nor in your dressing room, not in the foyer or the emptying auditorium. She was nowhere. And continued to be nowhere. For more than a year, it seems.

And now, you have a woman, with cheeks as lined as the Nile Delta, wanting you to find the someone you put in a box and promptly whisked into the unknown.

117

'I can see that you would…' you say. 'I would want to find – yes, I agree…' Your barrage of unfinished sentences does nothing to ease your own troubled mind, but perversely it seems to reassure the woman, who takes it as confirmation that you have signed and sealed her missing persons contract, and will, any time now, be finding her misplaced relative.

You feel the parchment of her fingers, the chill of her skin, as she hustles you forward. There is no escaping, and you allow yourself to be guided to the Green Room.

'So,' she says. 'What is the first step?'

And you wither. At her intense eyes and her expectant mouth. At her gusto and determination. All of which have left your own stage. You have not a single word behind your ear or up your sleeve which will fool, let alone satisfy, this most critical of audiences. There is only one trick she wishes you to perform – "The *Re-appearing* Lady" - and you scour your thoughts for a way – or an illusion of a way – to make this happen.

Despite your hesitation, she is grinning. And you notice an Ace of Spades, peeking from the cuff of her lace-edged shirt. And a single yellow bloom waiting to be produced from beneath her squashed black hat.

Her face slips from the benign; there is something diamond-hard in the light of her eye.

'Join me,' she announces. And she whisks off her gabardine coat, and turns it in a spin, revealing the purple cloak-like lining. And at the clap of her crooked hands a box – your box – appears in the centre of the room. She makes a show of tapping its sides, demonstrating its mundanity. You see what is coming. But you step forward nonetheless, like a witch to the stake, and climb inside. You have always been on the outside looking in. But now you are facing its tight walls and its dark limitations you feel its claustrophobia; you regret now the tasks you have asked of multiple others, all in the name of alchemy.

You hear the woman's tap-tapping on the box – either with wand or wizened finger - near your head. You feel the spin of your constrained world, turning your stomach like a storm-tossed vessel. And then … silence. No words from the outer-world; not even the lank-haired stagehand, whose tuneless whistling would be a gift, just at this moment.

So much quiet, but no peace. So much that you are emboldened. You push at the panel which you think is the door. The door which you think is a panel. You somehow insert yourself back into the world. Which is now a room filled with doves and rabbits and wilted flowers; with handkerchiefs and watches and three-card tricks. And, there at the sides, like wallflowers at a ball, are all the lost persons and lost souls. You scan the line, looking for the daughter. You think you spot her – the one in the blue striped dress. But your brief jubilation disappears in a wisp of smoke. Because the one thing of which you are entirely sure is that you have no inkling how to get yourself - or anyone's daughter - back from here. You recall the old woman's stare - realise she doesn't give a curse or 'cadabra for the lostness of everything you have ever made disappear. Just that you are her only hope of a daughter once more.

But Melissa is at your side. She is taking your arm, and, as music bubbles up from the floor, she whisks you into a polka. You clumsily follow her lead, spinning and turning round a room which has come to life, like a clockwork diorama.

She continues whirling and skipping until she manoeuvres you through a door that you are convinced was not there before. A green door, leading to an alleyway…

Without thinking, you step down in front of a tweeded gent, and produce a watch, as an encore, from behind his hairy ear. You are back on your stage, and for the first time in many a month, your artifice brings a flutter to your chest – the disbelief on the face of the man; the relief of the powdered woman whose watch you return. But mostly it is the vivacity which is now radiating from Melissa, watching your every move from the stage-side. You swoop a flower – a whole garden of flowers – from inside your jacket and present them to her smiling face.

Despite your daily deceptions and misdirection, you have no idea at this moment what the world around you is playing at. You have become the wondering and wide-eyed one, while your audience – and this woman in particular - receive your adulation.

When the hullaballoo finishes, and the auditorium seats begin to empty, Melissa saunters onto the stage and takes your hand. The hand which may or may not have performed an unbelievable piece of trickery. But never, you decide, has a performance of "Find the Lady" been more rewarding.

TOMORROW WILL BE BETTER

Beach winds are blowing, waves ruffled, showing off their lacy edges. She sits, observing all that is happening around her. The day is one for sitting at home, book in lap, hot chocolate, but some have braved the mood of the elements - gloves, scarves, glowing cheeks slapped by the wind. Brave grins at the battle they're losing with the weather.

She keeps her place on the rocks, even though their sharpness is stabbing her bones, forcing her to sit upright. The surroundings stir her desire to draw, to paint, but she contents herself with her phone, framing pictures of wind-tossed weed scribbled amongst the boulders. She picks out a pebble, an almost-rose traced in white marble on the charcoal grey of its rounded surface. She turns it in her hand, too good to throw into the sea; slips it into her pocket, finds another, hefts it, weighing its possibilities. She stands, re-arranging muscle and bone, and takes six paces to the edge of the foam. Far enough to keep her canvas shoes from darkening in the wet, near enough to make an impact on the churning waters.

She clenches her hand against tensed shoulders and heaves the red pebble.

It should have gone further, repaying the effort she has pushed into the throw. It should have travelled to the island sitting mistily on the horizon, but it goes only a few feet, drops disappointingly and disappears into the foam.

'Pull your arm back.'

Someone is there, someone she hasn't noticed. He talks at the sea, sneaks a glance at her, then bends to pick up his own stone. He says nothing, but his body speaks – like this, it says, pull your arm like me, it says, and you'll reach the island.

Never good at taking instruction, she doesn't want to be told. But it seems churlish to continue with things her own way. She watches again as he uncurls with another stone, and moulds her body into an image of his – not entirely mirroring, but an approximation of his bend and launch. To her disappointment, her stone goes further. He has been right and she is wrong. She wants to leave him to his perfections, but she can't.

'Challenge you?' he offers, weighing his next projectile. 'Winner buys hot chocolate.' He nods towards the kiosk sitting near the slipway begging for visitors.

'Shouldn't that be loser?' she wants to say, but she has been wrong once already. She searches for the stone that will give her the best chance, and tosses it from hand to hand, awaiting his word.

'You first,' he says, and she wants to ask how they will judge, who will have the final word. But she pulls back her arm and launches, little hope sitting in her chest. To her surprise the stone travels and travels, cutting through the misted air, dropping only when it seems that enough is enough.

He nods appreciatively, but without words. He draws his own bow arm, and she thinks of longbows pummelling the French. He is more warrior than diplomat she thinks, then stops her thoughts to watch the arc of rock, soaring, flying, before it dives into the deep.

'You win,' he says, clapping his hands together, maybe in congratulation, maybe to drum up warmth. 'Treats on you.' And he walks up the beach, dragging the shingle with his heavy boots, pushing against it so that she can see his calves outlined against his jeans. She follows, arms outstretched, trying to make the tip and bend of her body look deliberate, elegant. He waits at the top, holds out a hand. Her stubborn streak wants to climb from the stone pit her own way; but her

125

hand reaches forward, seeking the heat of his skin and the reassurance of another being.

They walk in step, accidently, but enjoying the balance of it all, until they reach the fogged windows of the café. He pushes the door and the colours of life seep out into the monochrome world they have inhabited.

She orders, carries the steaming cups, and hands him one, seating herself alongside. They embrace the warmth of their drinks and he reaches out a clasped hand; she meets it with open palm and he slips a stone - a perfect water-carved circle at its centre - wordlessly into hers.

He has chosen seats looking out to sea, looking to tomorrow. It will be warmer there, she thinks, than the stone-cold days which have gone before.

PAYBACK

'It's an epergne ma'am.'

'Yes, we all watch the Antiques Roadshow, Jackson,' you want to say.

'Fine, yes. Thank you, DC Jackson,' you say.

You look down at the curlicues of the silver centrepiece, now coated in a viscous layer of red gore. But your thoughts are interrupted once more by the young detective.

'They're used for displaying fruit, nuts, that sort of thing ...' DC Jackson is saying, in his Oxford-posh accent. He's been fast-tracked. In any normal story you would be wondering what you had done to deserve the Chief Commissioner's nephew on your team – the Chief Commissioner's entitled, arrogant nephew – but you know what you've done ... and you have to live with that.

'His name's Colonel ...'

'Mustard,' you want to say. 'Colonel Mustard, in the Dining Room, with the Epergne.' You look at the young man with his opinions stuck, like his nose, in the air, and his I-pad poised. 'Thank you, Jackson. Go and interview the scullery maid or whatever she's called.'

'Housekeeper, ma'am,' he says, as though she's a commodity every normal home wouldn't dream of being without.

You find yourself breathing normally again, once Jackson has left the room, even though you are now alone with the corpse of Colonel Mustard. You look at his face – ruddy, veined. A drinker, obviously. You try to keep your eyes away from the gaping gash across his skull, and look around for the pathologist who will root about in the poor man's pockets and find the one thing which will solve the mystery before Jackson returns with his electronic notes and his condescending air.

The door to the dining room creaks open a crack. A small face appears, and you jump up, not wanting any child to have to witness this appalling sight. As you approach though, you realise that this is not a child, but a petite angelic-faced woman.

'I'm sorry,' you're about to say, when the woman interrupts. 'I am Madame …,' she says, but with an accent so French that you struggle to make out the name.

'Mrs Mustard – Moutard,' you want to say. But obviously don't.

'The library, peut-etre?' She tips her head to one side, and you are taken aback by her apparent nonchalance. But you follow in her petite footsteps, and find yourself in an armchair, envying the fine collection of books which surround you.

Madame seems perfectly amenable to answering questions, and so, once you have expressed stiff condolences, you proceed.

'Was there anyone who …' 'hated' is the word you want to use. 'Held a grudge,' you say.

To your surprise, Madame splutters a laugh. 'Un – deux – cent,' she shrugs. 'You will find, Monsieur, that my husband was not an ami to many.'

You shrug yourself, enjoying the French gesture, deciding you will use it more often. After all, it will be Jackson who will be wading through two hundred possible suspects. You may be in debt to the Chief Commissioner, but you can take Jackson down with you as you go, you think, accepting Madame's offer of un tasse du café.

'Payback time' is how your jaundiced sergeant sums up the situation. And you can't help but agree with him … Now that you have heard of the Colonel's prejudice and bigotry and general vindictiveness to the world at large, and his family and staff in particular. Everyone has a motive it seems. Even the charming Madame – whose name it appears, is not Moutard, but Reynard. You wonder, fleetingly, whether limericks exist in France, and if so, whether you might create one with the near-rhyming names, to summarise this elegant crime scene. But Jackson's sour face puts pay to that idea, and you return to the matter in hand.

'Payback time indeed,' you say, looking through the mountain of motives in front of you. Take any one from twelve, you think. Spin a coin, toss the dice. Any one of these characters will do. You sympathise with them all, but the Commissioner is expecting at least one to be charged – and unless you want your own 'payback' to be settled with your skin – not to mention your career – you will need to put forward a credible case.

'Jackson – summarise the case for us, with your reasons for your particular top suspect.' You are aware that your instruction sounds uncannily similar to a GCSE exam paper. 'Good experience for your career,' you add, as you see words of protest beginning to form on his lips.

You can't deny he's thorough. And impressive. His reasoning is sound, and you like his choice of suspect. And the lad's hard work may get you off the hook with the Chief Commissioner. Because frankly, you have lost interest in Colonel Mustard and his intolerable lifestyle and outdated attitudes. You are glad he's met his Waterloo. But you see that bringing his slaughterer to book – and in double-quick time – will kill two birds. Crime solved, CC satisfied and therefore willing to let you off the hook. And maybe even three birds, you contemplate. If you can give a reasonable amount of credit to Jackson, he may be fast-tracked into someone else's orbit, and you will be left to return to your dusty office, and your old-fashioned typewriter, and a posse of ideas for your next novel.

Although that is what got you into this predicament in the first place – "borrowing" real crimes; borrowing real people. And most of all, presenting a barely disguised version of the Chief Commissioner – depicting him as a complete buffoon, to boot. Which of course he is. But for which you have paid dearly, by being given the direst of tasks, for many, many months. And the like of which you now know, you should never, ever, ever say or show or depict – EVER again. Because next time's payback could be far worse.

131

It could be Inspector Scarlett, in the Study, with the Chief Commissioner's belt – around your throat.

'Well done, Jackson,' you say. 'We'll make a detective of you yet.' And an idea permeates its way through your head. A story idea. A bestseller, perhaps. And maybe the biggest payback you might imagine. As long as you remember to change the names.

A CIRCLE IN A SPIRAL

It sounded pathetic – my reporting that "We seem to be in a spot of bother". Nothing of the finesse, the drama of "Houston, we have a problem". But at that point, when things first seemed to be going off-track, I didn't realise the enormity of the situation.

Up until then, you see, I had been careering round, happily orbiting the earth in sweeping loops, imagining the trail patterns I was leaving in my wake. But then, the sounds of motion – the humming and whirring and whining which ceases to be audible in the daily run of things – became stridently noticeable by their absence.

Luckily for me, there is a Norwegian and an Irishman on duty at the European Space Agency to deal with my call for help – because I'm not sure how my phrase would have translated into Dutch or Portuguese, and of course the French are always so obtuse when it comes to English idioms. But Inger and Ciaran, who had worked at the ESA for some years, take it all in their stride.

'What seems to be the problem?' Inger chips in.

I explain that my Specific Space Capsule seems to have stalled, even though the thrusters are still operating; I seem, simply, to be floating amongst the stars.

'We'll just check that for you, Charlie. Bear with us for a few moments.'

'I'm not going anywhere,' I joke, but Inger has already put our conversation on hold. I've completed all the projects allocated to me for my first solo flight, so I'm happy to sit back and let them check the technicalities at the Paris headquarters, confident they will shed some light on the possible causes and solutions for my predicament.

'Try XRJ6,' Inger comes back to me. 'Followed by a reboot of the aft reactor. That should do the trick.'

She sounds so incredibly self-assured, almost blasé, that I follow her instructions without hesitation. I flick the appropriate switches, and wait.

Now, sitting here in the eerie quietness of a star-studded cosmos, I realise that a few more questions on my part might have been wise. But I didn't, at that point, see the need. And so now

I'm just hovering, like a dragonfly over a pool on a warm summer's day, but without the ability to dart off at a moment's notice. And my thoughts drift to the last time I saw one of those remarkable creatures, with their translucent wings and their flashes of electric-blue. I had been sitting in my grandmother's garden, beautiful once but gone to seed, though still full of character and Englishness, with apple trees and honeysuckle, and hollyhocks taller than me. I was trying to relax, reading a tattered copy of 'The Invisible Man' on the decrepit bench by the pond, but her continual fussing - bringing tea and cherry cake, and wanting to know the ins and outs of my latest exploits at ESA - was frankly irritating. But now, as I sit in this half-set jelly of a situation, I find I am missing that fussing … and my heart squeezes a little at the thought that she's not around to hear about this latest exploit - this "spot of bother". No doubt it will be all over the six o'clock news, with dramatic pictures and flashbacks to Apollo 13, and I wouldn't want her to fret.

I try XRJ6 again, and consider utilizing XRJ5 and XRJ7, on either side. In my training, every switch and button had made perfect sense, had moved me rearward, onwards, spun me to any chosen angle; but everything seems haphazard now, the order of normal life flipped on its head. Had I been at home, dealing with a failed internet connection, I would have been jumping from device to device, flicking between screens and switches with happy randomness, despite my scientific background telling me I should know better. But now a prickling of concern is disturbing my equilibrium. I feel more than a little motion-sick, which is ironic, considering my stationary state.

Nothing changes. I'm not moving, but at least I'm not sinking or soaring either. I am – literally - in suspended animation.

'What seems to be the problem?' Inger asks.

I'm taken aback. To the extent that my sharp intake of breath must be audible down in the ESA. Am I just imagining that she's already asked that very question, or is it s*he* who has a sudden burst of amnesia? I hesitate, uncomfortable to be pointing out her error, and decide to explain my predicament again. Then I "bear with them" down in Paris, while they look into the problem.

'Try XRJ6,' Inger says, 'Followed by …'

'A reboot of the aft reactor?' I suggest, not entirely without sarcasm.

'Precisely,' she says, in her accented but perfect English. 'That should do the trick.'

And I know it won't. But I try it all the same. And I'm still sitting in my star soup, gazing at the spectacular views of the marbled orb which is Earth. Of course, it could be worse, I tell myself - out loud, because I have taken to talking to myself on this lonesome trek – so much worse. You could be on the M25, staring at the rear end of an Asda lorry, attempting to decipher the graffiti fingered in the dirt as you queue in stationary traffic for eternity.

For a while I am absorbed by the glory of what I am seeing, the sheer beauty of infinity, even though I've seen it over and over; unreachable and yet, it seems, only a metre beyond my fingertips. A memory of the telescope my father bought me when I was perhaps nine or ten comes hurtling into my mind; how furious he was with my mother when all she could do was to complain at the waste of housekeeping money. And, as if to prove a point, dad took me out to sit, night after night, in the darkness of the garden and observe the riches parading before us – Venus, Jupiter, more stars than I could even begin to comprehend - and I couldn't get enough of the vastness of that other world. It was that which had set my path, and eventually brought me to the Space Agency. And I wish now I had thought to tell my father that.

'What seems to be the problem?'

And we go through the whole experience again, like a dementia-induced conversation with my late mother, but on a grander scale.

It takes another three goes for me to realise that this might be it. That I might be stuck in this loop – in this kink in the space-time continuum, for that is what I have decided it is – for the remainder of my days. I can't say I'm not worried, because my stomach is tying itself into twists and knots – but I am not yet in a state of panic. I wonder, because of the repetitions of Inger and Ciaran, whether there is a similar hold-up in time, down there on earth. And if there is, is it occurring in the worst of situations? Nobody would mind, I ponder, being captured in time when they are in the arms of the new love of their life, or holding their new-born child; but what if I have induced a knot which is holding everyone in the worst possible of times? A home unendingly flooded, sodden treasures lapping to and fro at the water-swollen door. Or a forest fire which refuses all attempts to be extinguished. A voice forever trapped under the rubble of a bombed building. But I'm making myself morose. I force myself into a gravity-free flip, and tumble idly around the cabin. At least I can move within my motionlessness and I ignore Inger's seventh repetition as I somersault fit for Olympic gold. I contemplate those who might actually *deserve* to be held in this space aspic and my daydreaming wanders far and wide, but as I snigger at Andrew, squirming in his seat as Emily Maitlis asks for the umpteenth time "That is you, in that picture though, isn't it?", I hear Ciaran's gentle Kilkenny lilt, for once agitated.

138

'He's not responding. We're not making contact. We may have to ...' His voice fades, despite my desperate attempts to answer him, to scream for his attention.

And then there is nothing. I'm on my own, and I realise, with a weighty wrench to my being, that it might end like this. No matter how difficult the repeated lives of those on earth might be, they are not floating for eternity at the outer edges of the universe.

Still silence. I think of Sophie. And a sigh flutters like a flame-drawn moth in my chest. What will she be doing now? Like Grandma I hope she's not watching the news, but the thought of her, and our last words, formal, and stiff as starched sheets because of the argument we had picked at for over an hour on the night before I left ... and my eyes fill with tears. I want now, in this minute, to be home, to be holding Sophie in my arms, and telling her I'm sorry, that I will never ever argue with her again.

But still there is silence.

I look through my tears at the array of switches and buttons and screens in front of me. They all appear to be active, lighting and humming to themselves, but none of them are *doing* anything. They're not flashing error messages or even possible solutions. Frantically now I try contacting Inger and Keiran, or anyone at the ESA who will listen. I shout and blaspheme, find myself pleading, even the whisper of an unbelieving prayer, but none of it brings a reaction.

I close my eyes and think again of grandma and mother and Sophie. I can hear them all discussing and debating; they are such strong women and I know that none of them, in my place, would be giving in. I make myself look out. There, to the extreme left of my vision, is the blue sphere of the earth, where they are all present, in one way or another. I turn back to the panel, and locate the main switch. I flick it off, count to ten, and switch it back on again.

'What seems to be the problem?' Inger says.

GETTING THE BLAME

He shouldn't be there. And if he could see that, he couldn't understand why they couldn't see it too. His head lay on his forearms, resting on the table sticky with the fingerprints of a hundred previous felons. He tried to block out the droning voices; the endless questions stitched together with silences, intended, he presumed, to push him into uttering that solitary sentence with which he would incriminate himself.

The smell from the table - grease and cheap coffee and despair – got up his nose. Tom lifted his head, stared at his two inquisitors. The officers stared back, hoping that his movement was the beginnings of a confession, that their catch was floundering, that all that was needed was one final hammer blow before he gave in to the inevitable.

'Marie Hamilton,' the fat one said, sliding across a photo, contempt glazing his face. Tom made to put his head down again but they squeezed more words in too quickly. 'When did you last see her? She was a striking looking woman - you must remember?'

On and on, until his head was ready to implode.

'I told you.' His voice was weary. 'She's nothing to do with me – and I'm not in the habit of attacking strangers … specially women.' He returned the photo of the spectral blue face across the table. Leaned back, eyes to the ceiling where a solitary cobweb hung.

'Look.' The other one spoke so quietly Tom had to strain to hear. 'All we want to do is get to the bottom of this …' There was a sympathetic smile, as if kindness itself was being offered to him. 'But we need your help, Tom. Why don't we go back to the beginning – you tell us about that day, and we'll see if we can't untangle this whole thing …'

And he did go back, the pictures so clear, like a film playing over, that they hardly needed a word to explain them.

He was there, in his boat – "The Saucy Sarah" – rowing out on the rising tide, barely a ripple to disturb his thoughts. He'd gone on the pretext of catching mackerel, even though his chances were as slim as skate wings. It didn't matter. Out on the water he was his own man in his own world. No interruptions, no sound except the lazy waves slapping against the wooden hull. And he'd paused, looking back to the pencil-thin line of the shore, glad to have left behind his never-ending worries.

Tom had no idea how long he'd been out, or even if he might have nodded off; just that when he looked about him, something was different. Maybe it was the light - not skimming the water as it had before, but flashing, jumping, drawing his eye starboard. There, not a couple of yards away, was something which could have been a jellyfish or a bag of something worth having. Something about it made him take the oar, turn the boat. A game of tag ensued as he closed in - the thing bobbing away, toying with him. He leaned over, tipping the boat to its limit, then watched as the thing drifted on an unexpected ripple of water. Determined not to let it get the better of him, Tom tipped the oar into the sea and flicked. Eventually the scooping paddle threw the thing into the air. It arced above him in a perfect chain of droplets, and splashed, ignominiously, onto the slats of the boat.

It was no squid or jellyfish. It was a bag, clear plastic, tied with a thick knot. He held the thing up to the light, saw what looked like a handful of beads. He attacked the knot and wrestled the treasure free. It was though, rather than cheap beads, a string of very fine pearls.

'So, let me get this clear, Mr Putteridge. You sailed out, with no plans for your little trip, and *by pure co-incidence* you just happened upon a bag of expensive pearls?'

Tom had been as surprised as they were. His blank face would surely tell them as much.

'And, just to be clear, *again*, you then proceeded to smuggle them …'

'Not smuggling …' Tom corrected.

'But instead of handing them in at the station, you took them straight to someone who knew a thing or two about valuables …'

He'd gone to the Old Ship. He hadn't intended to, but his legs walked him in that direction. He'd sat at the bar with his pocket full of saltiness and pearls, and got into conversation with a man calling himself Jack Bridges.

'And this Mr Bridges, who you just *happened* to talk to, and who you just *happen* never to have seen before or since, offered you money … two hundred quid to be precise … to take said pearls off your hands?'

The man had bought him a few pints of Golden Stag, Tom told them. He'd been interested in his fisherman's tale; had offered to take the pearls off his hands. 'And that suited me just fine. I drank my fill of the man's beer, staggered down Quay Lane and was out for the count.'

'So – *according to you* – you saw no more of the necklace, from that moment on?'

Tom sighed. The repetitive questions and answers were becoming as stale as the air in the room.

'And you have no explanation as to how this poor woman …' again the photo was pushed across the table. The photo of the woman with the unholy bluish-white skin. '…came to have these marks …' A fat finger pointed to the perfectly round purple bruises decorating her slender neck. '…which match *perfectly* to a pearl necklace – not dissimilar to that which you were showing off at The Old Ship only hours earlier … How they came to be on Marie Hamilton's neck?'

'I sold the necklace. I told you. Marie Hamilton is nothing to do with me.' He was

145

indignant. 'You need to be looking for that man, Bridges …'

'But it was *that* necklace that was found at the scene…' There was a dramatic pause. 'With *your* DNA all over it …'

'But I've told you I handled it …I never denied that …'

'You did indeed, Mr Putteridge.' The fat officer paused to drink his cold tea. Tom felt a trickle of relief – they were listening to him at last.

'But what you haven't explained …' the man suddenly flourished his words like a matador's cape, '…is how Ms Hamilton came to have samples of *your* skin under her fingernails …'

Tom's trickle of relief became a torrent of anguish. They'd played him, and he hadn't seen those final words coming. It was obvious that they'd wanted to land the blame at his feet from the very start.

So, Mr Putteridge,' the quiet one started again. 'Perhaps we should go through what happened – just once more – but with the real version of events this time …?'

Tom sighed. How could he find another way to tell his story? He thought back to that night at The Ship. He had indeed found himself talking to Jack Bridges, had even shown him his haul of pearls. And it was while the beads were flowing back and forth through his fingers that that woman had sidled up.

'What an amazing find,' she purred, having overheard his story. 'I have a wonderful backdrop to set them off perfectly …' And her fingers had drifted down the valley below her neckline. Both Tom and Jack had been mesmerised, but it was Tom who had the temptation in his hands, and Tom who she beckoned away from the bar.

But it wasn't just the officers who were adept at playing Tom. Marie Hamilton had played him too, leading him on amongst the cushions and pillows of her boudoir, tempting the pearls from him, allowing her caresses to turn to deep passionate scratches before she decided to withhold her favours. An unforgiveable affront, and one which had Tom snatching to retrieve his pearls from her slender neck.

He hadn't meant to pull so tightly, to grasp her throat together with the necklace, but he was determined not to lose everything.

And there was something exhilarating about the reddening of her skin, the gurgle in her throat - more than just the act of retribution…

Before he knew what was happening, Marie had gone limp, silent, and the pearls had loosened from her neck.

And now he thought, as he looked from one officer to the other, he would need more than an elaborate fisherman's tale to unhook himself from this tangled net.

DREAMS IN A DRAWER

This story was shortlisted in the Wells Literary Festival Short Story Competition 2022

A letter came to your house last week. Such an unusual event.

Like most, you had long since blocked up your letter box – a source only of rattling and draughts you said. Because of course, they are obsolete - no use now for anything as out-dated as papers and postmen. Or visitors.

Books too are as extinct as leatherback turtles, but you were desperate to keep just this one and that – a few of your favourites, you protested, as tomes disappeared. And now you slide the few books off the shelves in dejected moments, which come more rapidly, more frequently, than they did. Not to read – you have a screen for that - but just to feel the memory of them sitting easily in your hands, to inhale their dry warmth and their comforting dustiness.

But we've forgotten the letter. No robin-red delivery of course, but a man in a suit, awaiting you when you peer round the door. He is turned away, scanning the horizon. He spins sharply at the sound of your presence, blinking over old-fashioned spectacles and a pinched nose, and you both stare, accompanied by the swallows in the eaves as you silently question each other's presence. Eventually he speaks.

'It seems this was mis-delivered,' he says, holding out a small paper square. 'And some time ago at that. We found it behind a bookcase – we're renovating.' As though their labours would explain, because he gives no further elucidation of what or where.

You put out a hand, but he seems reluctant to let the letter go, gazes at the envelope, like a friend saying a last goodbye. 'It's certainly taken its time to arrive,' he says, finally submitting it to your outheld palm. He wishes you good afternoon and is gone, before you can fully take in what has happened.

The letter is still sitting on your hand and, caught by a whisper of breeze, it seems to breathe as it gently raises and lowers. You fold your fingers round it, fearing it will disappear when it has only just arrived, and you carry it inside, taking it through to the kitchen and sitting it at the table while you make tea. You join it, cup in hand, and examine its detail; the writing is Edwardian you decide, with no idea why you are saying that. You follow the curling italics of the blue-black ink and see that the stamp has been applied on its side, as if the king were sleeping...

...and you realise that it is the monarch's portrait which has brought you to this conclusion. You have been without an hereditary ruler for almost as long as you have been without postmen. You abandoned William and even Charlotte at the same time as pens and papers.

You scrutinise the franking, which has only delicately touched the king, but is nevertheless blurred and indecipherable. No amount of turning and taking the square to the window reveals anything. You place it on the table and turn to your screen. Once upon a time your hand would have sought out the encyclopaedia on the shelf, but we've been over that already. You find King Edward – the one who followed Victoria, not the one who reluctantly followed his heart – and you note his dates, 1901 to 1910.

Nine years when the message could have been posted in a once-familiar red box, and another 120 years, give or take, for it to saunter its way to you. You hesitate, unsure about opening the door on something which has been minding its own business for such a time, but curiosity gets the better of you. After all, there is little excitement for you now, when all life is lived through that small screen. You have travelled the world, yet have been nowhere; you have seen every drama, every concert, every recital from that same solitary armchair. You vaguely remember visiting the theatre when you were young; you ponder the live music which surged through your chest, the colour and the spectacle interweaving you into that peopled world. Today, even with Advanced Reality, everything seems so very flat.

You rummage in the kitchen drawer, searching for something fitting to disturb the sleeping king and the long-forgotten message. There, at the back, you find the pearl-handled tea knife which might have belonged to your grandmother, or even her parents. Would that make them contemporaries of the king, you wonder, but your long-unused arithmetic fails to rise to the occasion.

You slip the blade between the layers of off-white paper, and slide out the innards, laying them, still folded, on the table.

The contents might be no more than an invitation to tea, you think. Yet it could be a proposal, a declaration, a plot to bring about the downfall of the rich and famous.

But you are getting ahead of yourself. You clear the table and take a seat alongside your new companion, holding out a hand of welcome.

My Dearest Evelyn

I hope I am still able to say that, after all that has transpired.

I hope we may still be friends, although sadly I realise now that it will never be more than that - which to me will be an everlasting regret.

I left your home in such great hurry on Thursday – I can only apologise again, and you will understand why. But in my haste, I left something behind, and I am wondering if you might be able to forward it to me? I know it is asking too much under the circumstances, but if I explain, then maybe you will take pity on me – just one more time.

You will remember that we talked so many times about 'Peter', that impish boy, and you often expressed a wish that there would be more of him - a sequel. I too was longing to tell more of that family's tales, and I particularly wanted to give more time to my beloved Wendy (who I cannot deny, has more than a little of your character in her).

So, some time ago I set out to write about the Darlings once more – but with perhaps a more adult perspective. Half the story was written, but I so wanted your opinion that I took the liberty of bringing it with me when I came to visit. I put it in one of your cupboard drawers for safekeeping, but in my rush to depart, completely overlooked it.

I am desperate to know that you still have it in your custody, and although it is more than I should ask, I pray you will have the compassion to send it to me at my London address. I don't think I have the spirit or the will to begin writing my tale all over again.

I await your reply in keen anticipation.
Yours
James B

You read those last paragraphs again. Unable to comprehend what you are seeing. Did some friend of Barrie – *the* Mr Barrie – dwell in this very house, where you spend your solitary days? And more significantly, had that same Mr Barrie left behind a manuscript, in your deserted, tired and uneventful home?

You stand, ready to turn out every last cupboard, thrilled at the idea of having not just a real book but an original manuscript in your hands. But you realise, as you sit once more, that of course things would have moved on – that the manuscript would have been sought out, that it would have been wrapped in twice-used brown paper, knotted and sent to the man's London address long before this moment when you have discovered its existence.

You pick up the letter and re-read it, slowly this time, urging your brain to put the simple facts in order. Only then do you see what the rest of us had already deduced – that of course the letter never arrived, was never in the hands of dearest Evelyn, because it is only now in *your* hands. And so she would never have known what you know

– about the book and its beginnings and its time in the cupboard at the top of your house, never to be finished because dearest Evelyn didn't know to rescue it.

You go and play hide and seek, amongst the fraying damask curtains and the yellowing linen and the unravelled wicker laundry basket. But do you find the lost manuscript? Because you must realise that is all the rest of us want to know.

You smile to yourself in the foxed bathroom mirror, and again at your reflection in the hall, before you leave the house. Your home is livelier now, warmer. Colours are emerging from beneath the dust and there is purpose in your step. You no longer sigh as you pass the old library building, stern in its red-brick suit, emptier than a hungry stomach. Instead, you lift your windswept shoulders in anticipation, heading for the Danish bakery where a handful of the past is presented in its windows. Two rhubarb and custard tarts please, and a bag of buns with sugar crystals sticking to their fat-bellied tops.

Lost boys need feeding and there is nothing like tea and cake, you agree with the grey-haired woman who twists and spins the paper bags. But then, in the square, you glimpse the gentleman who delivered the letter, sun reflecting angrily from his spectacles as he marches the streets. He halts, adjusts his coat collar and homes in on you like a missile. You turn away. But he follows, hanging on to your shadow. Something in his demeanour is telling tales on him and you shy away from his delivering words you never want to hear.

'She grew up you know …' Is that what he is saying? You step away, but his words skate around you like leaves on the breeze. 'There was a daughter – Jane…' you think you hear.

You cannot stop your ears from eavesdropping - but to enter into any exchange about the girl, Wendy, will surely break the charm. And so you keep walking, briskly, briskly, streets and alleyways and lanes, the trudge home stretching past its normal length.

You slam the front door like a fortress. You exhale with your back to the world, wanting only to cosset your secret inside the rooms of your house – just you and Wendy and the boys, sharing the buns and the pots of tea.

You have of course abandoned the wretched screen. Hidden it away in the cupboard drawer, for fear it might carelessly reveal to you the presence of a further volume - that Mr Barrie, despite his protestations, might have overcome his weariness and created again the contents of the precious bundle left in Evelyn's care.

Because you cannot conceive - if he has given further life to the family – what that would mean for your regular liaisons with them now.

Even if you were merely to have sight of such a book you are convinced that Wendy would surely know; that she would gather up the boys in a bundle and hustle them out of your door.

No. Their future must stay safely in dearest Evelyn's hands, wrapped and coddled in string and brown paper. You clutch the sugared buns, like babies, to your chest, as you settle into the cushioned seat by the back window, crooning as you scan the darkening skies for sight of the first evening star.

A CHANGE IN THE LIGHT

The silver dish is a barometer of Marcie's life. It was her mother's and has become dull, sitting on the shelf, unused. For too long it remained empty, but now it has accumulated a handful of coins, and Marcie considers this an omen - a sign that she should grasp what is available to her. She scoops up the money and heads out.

She looks like a duck, she knows that. Marcie's flat ungainly feet trip her up wherever she goes; she's convinced she's been built upside-down, her creator having been initially cautious, but then, having got to the end of her, found they had ample stock left, and had squeezed everything into her feet. She's found that if she colours her hair pink, ties it in pigtails – totally inappropriate for her age, but who cares - then people tend not to look down.

Marcie sings as she strolls down the street. "California Dreaming" is the start of her repertoire – she's an 80s girl who's stuck in the 60's. She switches to "Crazy" as she observes two women ranting, calling each other all sorts of f'ing things because one has taken the other's parking place. Marcie's glad she doesn't have a car. She replaces a box which has teetered off the wobbling tower being carried by the delivery man. 'Thanks love, you're a star.'

A star's good, she thinks, turning the corner and drifting to the baker's shop on the cobbled strip, looking longingly in at the window. But a star with a bit of money would be handy. Her mouth waters at the sight of cake, but particularly the tray of dark, fudgy, chocolate brownies. Marcie frequently thinks about applying for a job at a bakery … but they'd take one look at the nose ring, the candyfloss hair, and send her on her way. Anyway, she'd eat the profits and look even more like a duck, waddling her fat backside …

And then she notices the kerfuffle, further down the esplanade. More shouty people, wanting to claim their f'ing place on the bench with the best views of the harbour she thinks. But it isn't the usual entitled types. She strolls closer, humming "Dream A Little Dream", taking an apple from her bag as she stops and watches the scene unfurl.

Some fat bloke, maybe another bakery reject, is clinging fast to the statue of The Ancient Mariner – him with the extra-large duck bringing him down – while he's attacked by low-life. She knows it's actually an albatross – she's read the whole thing in the library, but sometimes it pays to play dumb.

The guys threatening the man drag him from the statue and throw him onto a bench, each glaring like it's a competition to be the most menacing. She imitates one of them, scowling, holding her fists to her chest, ready to spring. 'Piss off,' one of them snaps, a bit of spit leaving his mouth. She's too far away to worry, starts singing "All You Need is Love." 'F*** off,' the other one shouts, scoring a winning drop kick on the fat-guy's shin before stomping off. The other punches him, snarls, follows his mate. Marcie stands at the railing, watching someone on a marina boat wrap ropes into perfect circles on their deck.

'What did you do?' She says, turning to the bloke on the bench, biting every last piece of the apple.

'Nothing,' he grunts.

His hair is thin enough for the sun to have penetrated to his scalp.

'Y'head's burning,' Marcie says. 'Maybe you should move into the shade.' She indicates a tree near the kiosk selling coffee in paper cups. He doesn't respond, doesn't move.

'Didn't look like nothing,' Marcie says, watching the rope-tier again.

'It's *nothing*.'

Marcie notices his ponytail, wriggling down his back. His face is now as red as his scalp, and he rubs sweat from his forehead with the sleeve of his jumper.

'I'm fine, you don't need to hang about.'

'Nothing else to do.' Marcie smiles, throwing her apple core into the marina. Someone below shouts at her; she shrugs and waves, blowing a kiss. The man watches her, frowning.

'Fancy a drink?' Marcie asks; sees his open-mouthed face, corrects herself. 'Not a drink-drink,' she says, 'A coke – or a cuppa,' she indicates the kiosk. 'My treat,' she says, fingering the few coins in her pocket.

He shakes his head, reddening again.

'I'll go and order – take your time.' She sees him wince as he moves, holding his chest, coughing.

Marcie chooses a table under the tree and waits.

Eventually he comes over, and she indicates the seat next to her. But he's welded to the spot, pulling at the hem of the unravelling jumper. He seems about to turn tail, so she speaks up.

'Got you a Coke,' she says. 'You look too hot for tea.'

He picks up the can, slugs it back, his ample chin concealing his Adam's Apple. A trickle runs down the jumper before soaking in. He's looking anywhere but at Marcie.

'... they wanted my bike,' he's saying, but the words are absorbed, like the Coke, into his jumper. 'Wanted me to ...' His voice fades, and she can't catch what it is that the morons wanted him to do.

'So you weren't trying to steal the duck then,' she smiles, indicating The Ancient Mariner's bird.

'Albatross,' he mutters, but Marcie lets it go. They hold their silence, looking in different directions at the sea and the boats and the comings and goings of the marina. If they had to tell their story later, they would describe very different scenes.

He turns, replacing the can on the table. 'Thanks,' he says. '...find my bike,' he mutters.

'D'you need a hand?' She pushes aside her own unfinished drink.

He lifts his arm in a vague 'thank you' yet strides towards the station without an answer. Marcie watches him go, decides to follow; puts on a spurt to catch him up.

The pace is strangling his breath, but Bill needs to be by himself. His bruised ribs are protesting, and the jumper's too hot. He likes it though – hides a multitude of body he'd rather not think about. She was only being kind, he chastises himself, and all he could do was kick her in the teeth … not literally, but might as well have been. He hates all that tongue-tied and blushing stuff; walks all the faster to stop the thoughts.

His bike is where he left it, hidden in the bushes. He runs a hand across the saddle and down the frame. Caressing. If only everything were this simple. He's not up to swinging his leg over the crossbar so sets off, walking the bike down the path. It's comforting, in the afternoon sun – like walking with a friend. Except there's no conversation. And at this moment he'd really like that – someone filling the silences, making him smile. If only he could do the small-talk.

He slows as he reaches the bakery, checking the thugs aren't loitering for a second go. He looks in at the squared window – working out, if he were eating cakes at the moment, which he isn't, what would go into the square white box he would tie to his pannier rack. His mouth waters at the pillowy doughnuts and oozing custard slices. Then a voice arrives beside him.

"There a five million bicycles in Beijing." She is singing, for once forgoing her 60s vibe, following his gaze through the window.

'Nine,' he says.

'Sorry?' She looks at him, but he continues to stare at the window display.

'Nine million bicycles,' he mumbles. 'Well, in 1991 there were, when she recorded it – Katie Melua.' He's quiet again, just for a moment. 'So that would have been 2.5 bikes per household.' He waits for her to make fun, but she nods, continuing to hum.

He carries on, telling her about Beijing and the bicycles, as they start off down the road. He's not a man built for speed, but he notices that the woman has adjusted her pace to his. By the time they reach the park she knows that he likes Chinese food and cooks an 'okay sweet and sour', though he says it himself. The words aren't quite his own, and he smiles shyly. 'I'm Bill,' he says, holding out a formal hand.

'Marcie.' She returns the favour.

'We should have bought something – at the bakers,' he murmurs, not looking at her.

'Chocolate brownie would've gone down well with a cup of tea,' she smiles. Bill is disappointed at the implied criticism. He should have thought, should have returned her favour.

They continue walking, Marcie still humming. 'I've got biscuits,' she says brightly, stopping for Bill to catch up. 'Just as good – if not better – with a cup of Rosie Lee.' And she grasps the handlebar and helps push the bike up the hill to the place where she lives.

She will notice the silver dish, when she returns, looking brighter now, catching the day's light, and ready to be taken down from the shelf.

BELIEVING IS SEEING

We didn't notice he was gone at first – Uncle Gabe.

But there it was - the space left on the grass overlooking the elephant enclosure, where only minutes before he had been sitting with a tin of Golden Virginia on his lap and a Rizla paper ready to fill.

I've no idea how the tradition came about – either of our annual outing to the zoo, or of him coming with us, but every Good Friday Gabe would appear on our doorstep, nine o'clock to the second. While he read the paper, we'd pack a picnic big enough for a streetful of families, then squeeze into the Ford Cortina, the kids alternately giggling and moaning about who had the window seat.

After we'd done the big cats and the giraffe house and the reptiles, we'd find our way to that hilly bank of grass, spread out the travel blankets and unpack every last carton and bag.

Uncle Gabe had his own Tupperware box – Heinz Sandwich Spread on sliced white, and a flask of milky tea. Usually he'd reach over and sneak a slice of Simnel cake or one of Jodie's cornflake nests and shuffle back to his own spot - although on that day I didn't remember any of that. Barney was squealing at the sight of the elephant peeing like a fire hose, and all our attention had been drawn that way.

Gabe was with us … and then he wasn't. No sign of him ever having been there. All except a scorched patch, on the grass where he'd been sitting.

'Have one of you been messing around with a magnifying glass?' But in reality I gave little credence to the burnt grass, assuming it had been there before we came - some little urchin playing with a stolen lighter or matches.

'I'll have a scout round – for Gabe,' Pete said eventually, squeezing the last sausage roll into his mouth whole.

You're probably wondering why. Why we would go looking for a grown man, why we weren't just assuming he was sick of kids squabbling over chocolate biscuits and had gone for a quiet smoke somewhere. But that wasn't Gabe. Independence wasn't his thing. He didn't really socialise – and I'd assumed he was at his happiest when caught in the midst of our little family.

Pete went off with Barney trailing behind, and from the hill I watched them retracing our steps. I lost them behind the ape house, but then they re-appeared, Barney scouting left and right, Pete stopping to talk to someone with a badge.

'No sign,' he said, as they slumped back onto the grass. We all sat, unsure what should come next. To carry on our afternoon, mimicking chimps and orangutangs, seemed uncaring, but what else should we do? 'I'm sure he'll turn up – probably just gone for a pee.' We sat some more. A gust of breeze brought an odour of animal dung, and it hung thickly in the air around us. The kids made a fuss, pleading to escape the stink and go exploring; we gave in, with instructions to report back if they spotted Gabe. Pete and I scanned the pathways as we picked unnecessarily at leftover cake and crisps.

They came back, restless. 'When are we going home?' Lisa whined.

'We can't leave Uncle Gabe behind.' I sneaked a look at my watch. 'Perhaps we should check with the staff,' I said, noticing that the crowds had thinned, the sun was losing its fragile spring warmth. 'Just to be sure.'

There was an outbreak of shoulder-shrugging. 'I'll go to the ticket office – see if they can help,' I said. I hurried down the hill, checking every litter-strewn corner as I went. There was a queue at the desk and I waited while a man complained that he had paid two pounds ten shillings and now he was going to have to walk "*walk* - if you please*", to get to the lions, and what sort of deal was that? I fidgeted, slipping my feet out of my too-tight shoes, willing him to run out of steam.

I know this sounds strange,' I said, when eventually I got to the window, 'But we've lost our uncle.'

The girl with the cropped bleached hair stared at me, presumably thinking that this hadn't been part of the training. 'Have you tried the creche?'.

He's fifty eight,' I said patiently.

We were beyond the limits of her expertise, and she shrugged as she chewed her well-worn gum.

'Is there anyone else I can speak to?'

She picked up the phone and turned away. I heard the words "no idea" and an urging for immediate rescue.

'I'm Stephen, Customer Executive. What seems to be the problem?'

I wondered if the man who'd appeared at my side had promoted himself to his executive position, or whether it came with the armoury of keys clanking at his belt and the yellow kipper tie sporting a herd of red rhino.

'My uncle's gone missing,' I said.

'Okay. And what makes you think he's "missing"?' His fingers were only just resisting the urge to draw the inverted commas in the air.

'He …' My powers of description – either of Gabe or the situation – stuck to my tongue like peanut butter. 'He's not your average man,' I tried. 'Not worldly wise. He wouldn't just wander off – he always stays with the family. But he's been gone now for …' I checked my watch. 'At least an hour – more, probably. My husband's been round the whole zoo – there's no sign of him. We can't leave without him, but we can't find him…is there anything you can do to help?' I blurted the whole thing out, shocked to feel tears welling up. He must have noticed – Stephen – because he pulled a radio from his pocket.

'I'll get a message out to staff – get them to search their sections.' He took a breath, ready to launch into his message, then paused. 'What does he look like, your uncle – what's he wearing?'

Short, slim,' I began. Petite was the word you would have used for a woman; not appropriate perhaps, but it perfectly described his slight wiry frame, his close-set features. Even his teeth were small. 'He's wearing a tank top – orange, green, stripey … shirt and tie, suit jacket …'

I could see Stephen doubting the veracity of this, given the unseasonal sunshine of the day. But Gabe wore the same outfit whatever the weather.

"He's not gaga," I said, knowing as the words spilled out that they weren't right. "He works for Hawker Siddeley.' As if that explained everything. I'd no idea what he did for the aircraft manufacturer, but remembered him telling me once, quite indignantly, "I don't just count widgets. We made the Trident 3, you know."

Stephen opened his mouth, closed it, then clicked the radio into life. 'Attention all staff, we are tracking the whereabouts of an adult male …' and he continued with my description, word for word, and, to give him credit, not once smirking. 'Report back to CE ASAP, over and out.'

He glanced at me, apparently satisfied he had undertaken all actions befitting an executive.

'Thank you,' I muttered, unsure what should come next.

'Round up your family,' Stephen said, jangling keys. 'Bring them down here so that you're all in one place – don't want anyone else going missing, now do we?' He looked for the first time actually concerned.

I walked back quickly, knowing that everyone would be restless. But as I climbed the hill, a waft of Golden Virginia wandered into my nostrils. I sprinted the rest of the way.

'Gabe! Where have you been?'

Pete looked at me, attempting a whole conversation with his eyebrows. But I couldn't interpret.

'Kids – can you start packing everything up? Mum and I need to tell them that we've found Gabe.' Pete turned me firmly by the shoulder and walked me away.

'What the hell's going on?'

'You're never going to believe this – not for one single minute,' he said, striding us both towards the lake, where flamingos were gossiping on single legs.

'What? What am I not going to believe? Tell me, for God's sake.'

'Gabe says…' Pete took a breath. '…That he's spent this afternoon travelling through time …'

'Someone's switched that Golden Virginia for something stronger – I'll kill Barney if he's been playing tricks …'

'No, honestly – Gabe seemed really lucid. He genuinely believes he's been to the future and back in the last hour…'

And what makes him think …?' My thoughts as well as my hands were jittery. And was asking questions – giving the situation credence - making me as crazy as Gabe seemed to be?

'He says he went to London, and the streets were empty – not a single soul, everything closed down. He stood at Piccadilly Circus without a single car passing; Buckingham Palace, Big Ben, Tower of London – all completely deserted.' Pete skirted over my growing incredulity. 'Yep – and apparently Paris and Rome were exactly the same.'

'Well, all I can say is he's been to some pretty crazy sort of future," I said, 'Or more likely, he's completely lost it.' I stopped, gazing up at the sky, trying to find some sense in it all. 'I mean, when have you ever seen London without crowds?' I looked back at Pete. 'No, he's talking complete nonsense … d'you think he's had a seizure or something?'

'Maybe.' Pete rifled through his pocket. 'But he did give me these though – says he found one in the middle of the Champs Elysee and another in St Peter's Square.' We both looked at the tokens. 'Are these those new decimal coins they're bringing out next year?' I asked, giving no thought to how Gabe might have laid hands on them.

"Nah – it's got something about "Euro" stamped on it. It's some sort of football thing, I imagine," Pete said, turning them over in his hand.

With no other explanation, we both agreed that we needed to persuade Gabe to see a doctor – to get him checked out without frightening the life out of him.

He did have a check-up, and was given the all clear. Everything seemed to get pretty much back to normal. Time travel was never mentioned again, but we didn't visit the zoo the following year. Instead, we took a trip on a Thames river boat and there was only one hiccup – when Gabe said, in passing, "much busier this year", as we chugged past the Tower of London. I chose to ignore it, but Pete looked at me, raising an eyebrow.

The whole thing was forgotten, as family stories are, until recently. Until pictures paraded on television screens the world over – of cities as silent and empty as a pauper's funeral, as a pandemic swept through their streets. A shiver ran through me like an electrical charge. 'Pete, Pete – come and look. You need to see this.' I was frantic, pointing to the images. His thoughts immediately meshed with my own.

'Bloody hell … I don't believe it,' he said, looking at the deserted boulevards. 'You don't think … that he really did …?'

'Don't even go there Pete – this is completely bonkers...' But I was obsessed, watching the scenes over and over, contemplating the weird alignment between those images and the ones which Gabe had described, all those years before. He'd died, much too young, only eighteen months after the whole incident. But the urge was unbearable – to want to talk to him, to be able to ask him again about what he'd seen.

'When you spoke to him that day,' I asked, eventually turning off the screen, 'Did he mention *when* he thought he'd travelled to – what year it would have been?'

'I don't remember … but I didn't believe a word he was saying, so perhaps I wasn't listening properly….'

We both sank onto the sofa, allowing bizarre thoughts and images to wander through our minds.

'Do you think he really …?' we started all over again.

Suddenly Pete jumped up, went to the bureau and started turning out drawers, muttering to himself. Eventually he pulled out a twist of blue tissue paper and held out his hand.

Two one-euro coins.

'How the hell did he get these, back in 1970, unless …?'

'So,' I said incredulously, 'So, maybe …?'

We looked at each other. A long conversation without words.

'I wish he was here,' I whispered eventually. 'I wish we could … I don't know – apologise, ask him. I feel bad, that we doubted him …'

We both allowed our thoughts to wander once more. 'There's Prosecco in the fridge,' Pete said, eventually, giving me a hug. 'Shall we raise a glass?'

And so we did. 'Here's to keeping an open mind,' Pete chinked his glass against mine.

'And here's to the underestimated and very much misunderstood Uncle Gabe.'

TIED UP WITH STRING

It was raining heavily when the postman held out the parcel to her. A fat drip fell from the guttering onto the brown paper wrapping, dissolving the handwritten details.

'Thank you,' she called belatedly. Parcels and visitors did not find their way easily to Barbara Challoner's door; she did nothing to encourage them and they had no hesitation in returning the favour.

She was tempted to towel it down, but if she did, nothing would be left of any remaining details – and despite herself she was curious.

The door closed, bringing darkness once more to the hallway, and Barbara's attention fell to the package which she had not ordered. She eyed the string, debating the usefulness of unpicking the knots, but what use would she have for it, she thought, collecting scissors from an immaculate drawer.

The taut string crunched between the blades and sprung apart, releasing the paper. A book looked up at her, and she stared back at it with disappointment. The package was not hers, and must be returned; but although she flicked through pages and searched packaging, there was no indication of the sender.

Barbara picked up the book. She wasn't a reader, particularly of fiction, which she considered a waste of valuable time. "To Kill A Mockingbird". A title she'd heard of … but American, she sniffed, pushing the book away. It obviously wasn't for her, and as she prepared morning coffee, Barbara shook her head. It would be *her* responsibility, evidently, to deal with the misdirected parcel, and she sighed at someone else's inefficiency. But as she sipped the bitter brown liquid, she decided that, with no means of 'returning to sender' it *wasn't* her problem; she placed the book at the back of her cupboard where it remained untouched.

Until the following month. Four weeks, to the day – another rap on the door, another postman, another parcel.

'Young man,' Barbara barked, indicating the package. '*That* is not for me.' Her hands remained firmly clasped across her meagre stomach.

The postman stepped back, examining the neatly inked details in the weak sunshine, and thrust it back at her. 'Says number five here,' he said, looking from parcel to door number.

Barbara straightened. 'What name?' she snapped.

The postman tutted. He looked at the label and then at Barbara.

"Ms B Challenor',' he read, making the "Ms" buzz. 'That is you?'

'Well, yes, but …'

The postman shoved the package defiantly in her direction. Barbara turned to close the door.

But a lifetime of difficult customers had honed the man's reactions. He slid the parcel onto her doormat and whistled himself away.

'Outrageous,' Barbara shouted, 'I'll be putting in a complaint.' He waved without turning as he thrust his way past the hedge. Uninhibited by the passage of visitors, the shrub had stretched itself across her pathway, and she shook her head at the unruliness of both postman and greenery.

She looked at the parcel. The same neat wrapping, the same tight string, and most definitely addressed to her. She collected scissors

181

and again the brown paper sprang open; again there sat a book. This time "The Happy Prince" by Oscar Wilde.

'I *will not* waste any more time on this nonsense,' Barbara uttered, tossing book and paper to one side. 'And a children's book of all things – what am I supposed to do with that?' She walked away, pulling her old jacket from the hatstand and going to look for garden shears.

Within the hour, the hedge had been shorn almost to its bare branches, and seemed to shiver in the chill, but the activity had enlivened Barbara. Once she had consumed her Friday dinner of boiled cod and thin mash, she was drawn back to the new arrival. She held it up and fanned the pages, and this time a piece of paper fluttered free.

```
        Thomson and Henry
Independent Booksellers, Taunton
        - with compliments
```

There was an address and phone number. The mantel clock was chiming six, but Barbara picked up the phone and dialled nevertheless, hoping there was someone left in this world with the same work ethic she had maintained, despite being forced into retirement.

'Oliver Henry – can I help you?'

'I've received a package from you - a book.'

'Is there a problem?'

'Evidently. I didn't order it. It's not mine.'

'I'm sorry madam. Is it incorrectly addressed? …'

'No.' Barbara interrupted. 'The address and the name are mine – but I didn't order it. I've never ordered anything from you … I don't read books.'

There was a silence, as if the bookseller were struggling to comprehend such a person. 'I see,' he said eventually. 'And what did you want to do with the book, madam?'

'Well, if you tell me who sent it, I'll return it to them …'

'I'm afraid that wouldn't be possible, madam. Data protection and so on.'

Barbara sighed heavily at the mess the modern world had got itself into. 'In that case, I'll bring it back.' She huffed, replacing the phone indignantly.

She irritably contemplated her predicament as she put a bare sprinkling of leaves in the pot, and sufficient water for one cup. 'So now it's my responsibility to return this book – these books - to Taunton,' Barbara muttered, contemplating the wait for a bus which would inevitably be late, and filled with people coughing and talking too loudly. She switched on the radio, hoping for a documentary; but it was a play, all jangling music and tearful voices. She flicked it off. She'd already finished last Sunday's paper which she normally made last the week. An early night then, she sighed, turning out lights, before slipping into her winceyette nightdress.

But she tossed and turned, too hot, too cold, watching the dark hours slide past. Morning brought a lightness to her bedroom. She went to the window and groaned as she saw the snow. There would be no trip to Taunton, and Barbara realised that a part of her was disappointed. She was tempted to slip back under the eiderdown, but instead castigated her own slovenliness and forced herself to dress, pulling on extra cardigans to save on heating.

The radio was full of overblown weather reports and stranded cars. 'Foolish people,' Barbara muttered, as she buttered toast more generously than usual. She switched the news off, but the silence of the blanketed street had pushed itself inside the house and weighed heavily on her shoulders. As she scanned the room, her eyes fell on the cupboard where she had banished the books. She huffed. Well, it might pass an hour, she thought. She reached for the one with the mockingbird on the cover.

When Barbara looked up again, three hours had run away and the world was swathed in winter gloom, apart from her lamp. She pondered why someone would think a story about a black man in the Southern States of America appropriate reading for a woman like her … and a criminal at that. But questions kept popping into her head. Why had the lawyer – Atticus Finch – put himself out to represent such a man? And why had he encouraged his children to be so … so what? she considered. Tolerant, kind? 'It's only a book,' she found herself saying, and switched on the evening news to push Mr Finch and his children out of her head.

By lunchtime the next day she had come to the end of their story. As she closed the cover, Barbara was conscious of the empty chairs, the stillness of the room. It unnerved her to realise she was actually missing Scout and Jem Finch. 'It's only a book,' she muttered again, retuning the radio to a classical music station to sweep away the characters.

The snow continued, obliterating the sky and any remote chance of going out. No unread newspaper, no radio worth listening to, Barbara wrapped her cardigan around her body and dozed. She chastised herself severely when she awoke, alarmed that she might end up in a care home if she allowed herself to slide down the slope of old age in this way. She forced herself to do the ironing, but her mind wasn't on it, and she almost scorched her best cream blouse. When nothing was left unpressed, she scoured the room for something else to occupy her – and eventually her hand went to the cupboard again, and pulled out Oscar Wilde.

She stopped only for tea, thinking as she filled the pot, about the prince who had given away his riches, wishing inexplicably that she had a humble toasted teacake, and someone to share it with. She reprimanded herself, and continued to read – this time about the selfish giant, sharing his garden. Barbara glanced at her own plot, wondering about the last time anyone - including herself - had enjoyed it.

The two books sat on the table. The snow had cleared, and Barbara had no excuse for not returning them to the bookshop – except that she had read them now, and they might be considered second-hand. But the shop really ought to be able to throw light on their sender, she thought, and so she made her way to the bus stop, surprising Mr Blundell – and herself - by calling out good morning.

Mr Henry, whom she had spoken to previously, was apparently absent from the shop, and Barbara's heart sank at the thought of having to relate the saga of the unordered books yet again. But a young woman with green-tinged hair was asking if she could help, and there was nothing else for it but to retell the tale.

'Let me just check something,' the girl with 'Natalie' on her badge said breezily.

While she waited, Barbara wandered around the shelves, noticing titles she had read as a girl, but so many more stories sitting with them now, just waiting, like orphaned children, for someone to choose them.

Natalie called her back to the desk. 'So sorry to have kept you ... it's all a bit strange really ...'

'What is?' Barbara barked, when the girl hesitated.

'Well, it appears we've been asked not to disclose the details of the purchaser. However,' she continued before Barbara could interrupt, 'We are able to say that there will be another ten such deliveries – one each month – and that, if you can "demonstrate" that you have *read* each of the books by the end of that time, then more information might be released to you ...' She looked up at Barbara as they both considered what might happen next.

Barbara found herself sighing. Loudly. Being told what to do, particularly by "persons unknown" was not something she was able to take lightly – in fact, to take at all. 'But I don't read books,' was all she could manage to say.

'Well, perhaps …' Natalie was obviously searching for the most diplomatic way to say what she was thinking.

'Let me save you the trouble,' Barbara butted in. 'What you want to say is "stop making a fuss – it's only one book a month, and there are far worse things happening in this world which you are not being asked to endure" … is that about the sum of it?'

Natalie nodded. 'Well, yes…' she paused. 'And, can I add that … you might actually enjoy the experience …?'

Barbara recognised a stalemate when she saw one. She was going to get no further information – or sympathy for that matter – from Natalie, and there was no Mr Henry available to make further representations to. She wandered around the shelves, unsure what she should do next. There was lively chatter at the back of the shop, people pulling off scarves and asking after each other. Barbara looked on, with a slight pull in her chest.

'It's our book group,' an assistant stacking copies of the latest Robert Galbraith on a table told her. 'They meet here every month … they're looking for new members … if you wanted to join …' His voice faded as he saw the expression on Barbara's face.

'Oh no,' Barbara blustered, 'I don't read books.' But as the words left her mouth, she thought of Atticus Finch, and the Selfish Giant; and an image of Boo Radley inexplicably came to her - a misfit, yet there to help others when he was needed.

'Well, maybe I'll stay for a while,' Barbara said. 'Just ten minutes perhaps … see what goes on …' And at that moment, she realised she was hopeful that the ten additional parcels might indeed arrive at her doorstep.

TAKING SIDES

1971

The girls giggled as they paddled up to their knees in the shallow waters of the Blackwater River. The sun caught the bellies of the water droplets as they cascaded from their splashing fingers, creating fleeting necklaces around them. This was their summer, their last summer before they became women and had to put aside such foolish things; and in this moment the strength of their friendships was knotted tighter than ever.

Kate, who would soon become Katherine, waded her way up the shallow bank, wrapping her dress above her knees, missing the sash which trailed in the lapping water. She threw herself onto the picnic blanket and called to the others.

'The butter is running from the sandwiches girls,' she laughed, 'You'd better come now, before our feast slides into the river.' She moved two bags into the shade of the elegant willow. She wrang out the soaking ribbon on her dress, and as she did so, a call came from the bridge a few yards upstream.

'Katherine Hennessy – what in the name of God are you doing without your shoes, and your dress up around your backside?'

A deep breath for fear of her father; but the hearty laughter which followed revealed it to be only Jack, her brother, doing a passable impression of their parent. She looked for something to throw in his direction, but it would have been a waste of good food, and anyway he was already clambering down to share their idyllic spot and their lunch.

The shouting had brought the other girls to her as well.

'I'm ravenous – a hundred times more than ravenous,' Nuala said, parking herself on the edge of the blanket and attempting to dry her feet on the parched grass, but succeeding only in decorating her soles with shreds of greenery.

A figure wandered behind Jack, unsure of his place amongst the camaraderie. Katherine looked past her brother, and then back to his face. 'And who is this, that you've brought to see us and not had the manners to introduce?' she raised an eyebrow, but was unable to keep the smile from her lips.

'Stephen – come on now. Come and say hello to my gobby sister. She won't give me a minute's peace until she knows all about you.'

Stephen came forward two steps, but still far enough away not to be within touching distance of any of the girls.

'Oh come and sit with us man,' Katherine beckoned. 'Or you won't get a look-in with the food – not between Jack and Nuala here, who could eat a horse and still be looking for afters!'

The boy sat on the edge of the blanket, reluctantly taking a sandwich or a biscuit or whatever else was passed in front of him, blushing with a ruby glow beneath his freckles every time he was spoken to.

'Katherine made those cakes, so I wouldn't be even taking a bite if I were you,' Jack jested, howling as his sister pulled at the hairs on his arms, where muscles were beginning to blossom. But Stephen was still looking at Katherine's face, long after it would have been polite to look away. He was gazing as though he had never seen a female before, as though she might have stepped from the Renaissance painting he had seen in the foyer of the library building when he had been taken for a day out to the city.

Talk began again about another dip in the river, but two of the girls – Christine and Siobhan – were pulling shoes onto still-wet feet. 'We have to go – you know what the parents get like if they think you're up to no good. As if we couldn't already have been up to all sorts of mayhem in the time we've been here,' they laughed. Waving and shouting goodbyes, they reluctantly drifted away.

'Me too,' said Nuala, pushing herself up from the grass, attempting in vain to scrub a green stain from the hem of her dress. 'No peace for the even vaguely wicked in our house,' she laughed, 'And church to attend in the morning, before the dawn has even cracked.' She pulled a face, and was gone.

Leaving just Jack and Katherine and Stephen. And then just Stephen and Katherine.

'Would you fancy a walk?' he asked, getting to his feet, indicating the path alongside the river.

Kate pulled on shoes and tucked her wild hair behind her ears, attempting to look something like respectable.

They talked – tripping over their words at first, but then found their stride, speaking of songs and books and places in the world they would travel to when it was no longer down to their parents to decide. They stopped and watched a family of ducks, little ones trying to clamber the muddy bank and succeeding only in sliding back into the water.

'Did you ever see "The Great Escape"?' Stephen asked, laughing at the failed attempts of the birds; and their conversation turned to favourite movies and the best scenes. Their tastes in everything, it seemed, ran in the same directions, and anyone looking on would have thought they had known each other for years. Their eyes didn't leave each other's faces, and their fingers touched tentatively, like the leafy branches arching overhead.

'Well, when we've filled those piggy-banks fit to bursting, we'll meet at the airport, the two of us – the year after next, d'you think? And we'll find ourselves a place on the banks of the Seine and toast each other with a bottle of something …St Emilion I've heard is a good one!' Katherine laughed. Then looked from Stephen to her watch and reluctantly turned back towards the picnic spot. She began packing the last of the food back into the bags. Stephen took them from her without being asked, and something inside her danced a little beat. They turned and clambered the bank towards the bridge. Without thinking, Katherine turned to the right, towards the busy streets on the same side of the river. At the same time, Stephen turned to the left.

Neither had thought, both had assumed.

'But I thought – you're a friend of Jack's – that you must be …' Katherine shook her head.

'Jack never said. We talk all the time – but he never said …'

They looked at each other, diving into the pool of gentleness in the other's pleading eyes.

'Why?' The question hung there, the one question they hadn't discussed amongst the hundred others they had spoken of, and all they wanted was to forget about the bridge and who's side was whose, and who thought what, and who really cared, because no-one was right.

And what would happen if either of them took the other home – Protestant to Catholic, Catholic to Protestant? And they stood, fingertip to fingertip, a hundred silent conversations buzzing between them like telegraph cables, before once more turning on the bridge - she to her side, and him to his.

A DEAFENING SILENCE

A February beach. Never the place for children, particularly as varied as this clutch were. Jessica, struggling to manage the tentacles of teenage years, sulked at the refusal of ice creams. She had set her sights on a raspberry ripple and salted caramel ensemble, and was ready to argue until the tide ceased to turn.

Daniel was the stoic, the middle child who had long since abandoned attempts to please a dominating older, and a manipulating younger, sibling. He had found his own path, and was focussed on treading it, come what may.

And then Leo, the late blossomed, clutching the benefits of babyhood far beyond physical reasonableness. He hogged his mother's lap and attention, excluding all others with alternate tantrums and endearing grins, and, when all else failed, sending fat wet globes of tears chasing down his cheeks until even the hardest heart had to give in.

Without paddling and inflatables and beach balls and candyfloss, entertaining the tribe was a difficult affair. But the previous evening, father had spotted two articles in the Western Daily News. One which he had shared in surprise with his wife, and one which had inspired him; it was this second which had provided him with a plan which he was determined would banish the sulks and disapproving sniffs of his children.

'It was found here – along this line of coast,' he said now, peering beneath a searching hand. Leo was pre-occupied with an act of cuteness in front of an older woman exercising her border collie on the sands. It might yield results – sometimes a sweet, at best a coin to treat himself. He hadn't heard his father's words. Jessica's arms were crossed against the world; her hands were engulfed in the cuffs of her sweatshirt, and her bottom lip was bitten to rawness by her scowling. But Daniel, with his boots and spade, was willing to give his father the benefit of the doubt.

'What? What did they found – find?'

'A message – all the way from … Australia.' Father produced the final word, like a rabbit from a tattered hat.

A boy who had known only mobile phones and electronic media since his youngest years barely batted an eyelid at this information. But there was something about his father's continuing scan of the waterline, and the fact that he had, for once, exclusive parental attention, that made Daniel take note.

'How did they find it here?' - the lack of any sort of electronic device surely making the event unlikely.

'A message, in a bottle ...' Another rabbit out of the tattered hat.

Daniel took some convincing that this would be someone's preferred method of communication, but the idea began to grow on him, and enthusiasm gradually blossomed on his solemn face.

'There might be another,' father ventured. 'The story goes that they sent more than one ... and if one was found here, than it stands to reason ...' He allowed the story to hang in the salty breeze, waiting for someone to catch it.

'I could look,' ventured Daniel, wielding his long-handled spade. And he wandered along the wavering line of water, as if to demonstrate his seriousness in the mission. Every few moments he would stop, kick at the wet sand with his boots, and stab an experimental spade's depth into the shifting shore.   After ten minutes, he had unearthed a broken limpet shell, a teaspoon and a smoothed and polished piece of green glass. He picked it gingerly from the sticking sand and looked disappointedly at his father. 'This might have been it,' he said, thinking of the beer bottles and wine bottles he had seen lined up in the recycling bin. 'This might have been their other letter,' he said despondently.

'Maybe. But I'm sure they'll be more. Worth another look.'

And then, there it was. Daniel was fighting the waves for something, heaving at the ground as though he were battling a sea dragon. 'I've got it, I've got it!' he kept screaming. And that of course brought Leo in an instant. Even Jessica deigned to saunter over, glancing over her shoulder as she pretended to look out to sea.

The bottle, which father had planted earlier, was held aloft by Daniel, brandishing it like a grand prix winner.

'Well done, mate. Just need to try to get it open now – see what their message is …'

But father's words were lost in the wet spume-filled air as Leo squealed. 'I want one – I want a bottle …'. On and on.

'Why don't you just go and look for one?' Jessica butted in unexpectedly, tired at last of the little brother's insistence on possessing everything of everyone else's. 'Go – scram,' she snarled, as Leo began throwing sand at her legs.

All attention had been stolen away from him as Daniel worked at the bottle top, desperate to read the Antipodean message, and so Leo took himself in his slopping red wellingtons further up the beach. He swung his spade conspicuously at the sand – here, there, random grandstanding efforts, but no-one was buying his calls for attention. He dug a hole, half-heartedly. He dug another. And then. And then …

'I've found it! Buried treasure!' he shrieked, as he continued to dig. 'It's a rocket,' he declared. 'Mum, mum – I found a space rocket – look!'

Mother had returned from her foray to the shops - her search for something warmer than her best holiday clothes, which she had inadvisably brought with her. She looked up. She heard the harsh clank of metal on metal. The evidence supporting Leo's claim. And the thought dripped into her brain; the article Sam had read to her the previous evening. And there the thought detonated.

'Come away!' she screamed, running in slow-motion through dry sand. 'No, Leo, no …' as the child continued to batter the metal object with his spade.

But her words were swallowed by something a thousand times more powerful.

The world continued to turn – the lights on the arcade machines continued to flash, the smoke and steam from the old-fashioned train hung in the air; the dog chased the ball across the beach; the seagulls swooped and circled. But there was no electronic music, no hoot or hiss from the engine, no barking from the spaniel, no squeal from the gulls. The silence was thunderous.

The first newspaper article which had taken father's attention now flashed it headline large in his head. "WW2 unexploded bombs found on South Coast". Mother was long past such prompts; her gut had already churned the panic and adrenalin that was pushing her across the sand. Father turned in silent horror, unable to move either one foot or the other; Daniel too watched the cinema of events, having no notion though of what was playing out before him. It was Jessica, string-thin and lithe and full of the undeserved fitness of the young, who sprinted to Leo, and yanked him, lifted him from the wet sand, ignored his red boots depositing themselves on the beach. Who ignored the boy's silent wailing, his soundless demands for his spade and his space ship.

As she deposited the brother on the promenade, continuing to drag him on his little legs towards the harbour, she looked over her shoulder. Mother had taken Daniel's hand and was moving faster than her daughter had ever seen; father though was still welded to the spot, looking from the recently dug hole to his family and back again.

Jessica stopped, breathless now, and aware that she was crying. She glanced down at the still-protesting Leo, and then across the empty sands to her father – her beloved father, she realised, the father who still spoke to her when she sulked and snapped and argued. Who occasionally slipped a small bar of chocolate onto her cluttered desk, holding a conspiratorial finger to his smiling lips. And she cried out to him. And this time the silence was broken. Her unexpected voice shattered it into a thousand pieces, and the impact of those pieces jolted her father. He jerked as though a thunderbolt had found him; she could see him forcing his legs, pushing against the shifting sand. But moving so, so, slowly.

Mother and Daniel arrived on the promenade, panting and grinning awkwardly with relief. At the sight of them, Jessica roughly shook away Leo's hand, leaving him wailing once more, and despite her mother's screaming, sprinted towards her father.

Five seconds; ten. And then the silence was truly ended.

STANDING RIGHT IN FRONT OF ME

It was a thought which had returned to me again and again – the suggestion that it was possible to bring a person back to life, just by remembering them.

Of course, I knew it wasn't true. Dead is dead, right? Once you've seen that coffin slipping through the curtains, once the strains of the final music are fading and you are headed for the display of wreaths and the condoling words of near-strangers, then that's it – get on with life, on your own. That person is, at best, a fading photograph on a dusty mantelshelf.

But it was one of those "what ifs", which returned to me when sleep was doing its best to hide behind the wardrobe; and it dragged with it a bizarre and long-unvisited thought – that I really wanted to talk to my mother; because there were few others I would trust to be frank on the subject, and mother had always been nothing if not brutally honest.

And in reality, there was no-one else, full stop.

Because I'd tied myself up in a tight web of what I liked to think of as self-sufficiency, but was in reality a desiccated recluse's life. I would allow no-one to get near me – physically or emotionally – gradually pushing away all the friends we'd had when Ffion was alive.

I'd alienated family particularly. They'd tried so hard to help at the beginning – the sister who'd baked and bolognaised for me; the brother who'd urged "Come for a pint, Simon; join us in Greece, Simon", but nothing had tempted me. In fact, it had made me worse. The thought of sitting at their tables, the only singleton amongst smug couples and storybook families, was the very thing to make anyone newly alone feel a hundred times worse.

And they would have wanted me to talk about Ffion. I couldn't. Not only could I not bring the words to my lips, they wouldn't even form in my thoughts – I wouldn't let them. The only way I could deal with her not sitting in her chair or standing at the kitchen table - listening to a radio play while she made a hash of rolling pastry, but managing to produce a topsy-turvy pie that tasted amazing – the only way I could deal with her empty spaces was to wipe her existence from my mind. Don't talk about her, don't look at pictures of her. And don't, whatever you do, open the wardrobe door and see her clothes hanging there, like a passing glimpse of her as she moves between friends at a summer lawn party. Just keep her at bay, as though you had never met her and never heard her sunny voice, or woven your fingers through the lively curls on her head, or held her in your now-empty arms. No. Do-not-even-think.

What I wanted to ask mother about was the nagging insistence of those words. Would it work - if, just once, I allowed Ffion into my head, would she re-appear? Was she holed up somewhere, waiting, impatient at my not bothering to recall her into my life? 'How much longer am I going to have to sit here?' I could hear her teasing, as she swigged from a glass of something cold and laughed at the ridiculousness of the situation.

But mother was gone as well. Not dead you understand, not this time. She had decided that my father and all her children were just too bothersome to deal with. She had always been a free spirit, happiest painting bizarre abstracts on vast canvases which overtook the upstairs of our house. She too had stopped talking to people – "they eat up too much of my valuable time" - and had shut herself in the attic. But of course, young children are no respecters of privacy, and we would clatter up the bare wooden staircase and pound on the door. Or, worse still, march right in, slipping on the paint which had slithered its way out of tubes and onto the floor, charging into paintings which would otherwise of course have been accepted by the Royal Academy, a fact mother never ceased to tell us while she tried to repair our clumsy damage.

One day when we came home, she just wasn't there. And I'm not sure if we were pleased or disappointed. It didn't seem to affect us that much - she'd never been the one to provide paired socks, or cake, or a place on her lap when we'd fallen.

I'd never heard from her since – just an odd scrap of gossip on a street corner, snipped abruptly short when I was near enough for embarrassment to set in. But I knew she was the one person who would be honest with me – who would strip away the common-sense from the notion of conjuring the dead, and launch into the serendipitous world of artistic possibility. I needed to find her. And having done so, I might then be able to find Ffion.

I typed mother's name into the search-engine, expecting her to be the first subject to appear on my screen. But it was apparent she hadn't achieved the fame she had always felt was her due. I scrolled on, eventually finding her on the third page of results, pictured with canvases I'm sure had been at our house in my youth. There was also mention of her at an obscure gallery in Tenby.

It had been so long since I'd been away, since I'd done anything different in fact, that I had to search my thoughts before I could search the house, in pursuit of the things I might need. In the end I took only essentials – toothpaste and brush, underwear and a notebook, two notebooks. I hadn't acknowledged it out loud but the notebooks were my security blanket, especially the purple calf-leather one, which I had never wanted to write in, but just carry clutched to my chest, in case a wonderful idea might manifest itself - on a muddied pavement, or a bus to Tower Bridge. I added a sweater for good measure, and slung the bag over my shoulder. It was only when I reached the station that I realised I had no idea how to get to Tenby. Did it even have a station?

A patient woman behind the finger-marked glass of the ticket office talked me through and took a ransom of money in exchange for a meagre ticket. But it was my gateway to finding my mother, so I accepted the situation and followed her instructions.

After rocketing fast trains and slow stopping trains I found myself overlooking the bay - somewhere which had found its way from a picture book, with its pastel range of houses and its curve of yellow sand, and boats bobbing as they were want to do in books. I asked the nearest person for directions to the gallery but they returned my questions unanswered. I tried another with similar response, although this time they pointed to a sign at the end of a narrow passageway. Tourist Information.

It appeared that the gallery was on the outskirts of town. I slung my bag back over my shoulder, weary now in the surprising heat of a Welsh afternoon, but ready to follow the directions.

The gallery was almost anonymous, hidden as it was between a Fish and Chip shop and a local supermarket with towers of plastic baskets tottering outside its windows, barely restraining their tawdry contents. But find it I did, and went straight to the door, pushing hard against its dust and grime.

And there she was. Not hard to find at all it turned out. Sitting at the back of the shop with cigarette clouds burgeoning in front of her wild, unruly, but ultimately recognisable hair. It had been orange the last time I had seen it, but now the purple streaks fought with the grey.

While I had dragged childhood pictures to the forefront of my mind, she apparently was unable to do the same. She stared through the screen of nicotine, appearing only to assess my ability to afford any of the questionable paintings which covered the walls. She was struggling for an opening line, and so I spoke out.

'It's me, mother. It's Simon.'

I might have announced myself as Beelzebub or the tax inspector. She swivelled on her chair, seeking out exit routes.

'Simon,' I persisted. 'Your son?'

Perhaps she had been about to deny any such existence, still turning this way and that. But then her chin dropped. She slid off the high stool, scrunched the cigarette into a saucer and came towards me.

I wondered when you'd come,' she said, slipping her arm in mine as though she'd been doing it since I'd been tall enough for it to be possible. She flipped the "open" sign and pulled the door to, leading me along the unkempt road. I hesitated when we reached a grimy café, but she laughed and moved to another, marginally more respectable, a few doors down. Mother waved to the proprietor, ordering without asking, as though I were still a boy with too little sense to know his own mind. Then she looked me in the eye. 'Is it money?' she asked, opening her arms as if to display the wealth of riches she'd accumulated and from which I might select a lifetime of treasure.

'No.' I hesitated. It was difficult now that I was facing the reality of a mother who had never been ordinary, not even in my wildest dreams. 'I wanted … your opinion on something.'

She looked neither surprised nor nonplussed; merely swallowed the thought alongside her tea and buttered teacake, which I knew I would be paying for. 'A woman – it's usually a woman,' she declared, licking the grease from her stained fingers.

'In a manner of speaking.' And I let it all out, like the oozings of the paint she had splattered randomly in that attic room. I told her of my life with Ffion, the betters and the worse, and particularly the sickness. Mother nodded at intervals, nothing seeming to phase her.

'So – in your experience,' I finished up, 'Is it true? Can you bring someone back to life – just by remembering them?'

She contemplated. She rummaged in her worn leather bag and pulled out a cigarette packet, then, remembering where she was, replacing it. She pulled a starved purse from the same cavern and placed it on the table. 'My dear,' she said, and I thought it was I who was about to be asked for money. But to my shame and relief, mother began to speak with more wisdom and authority than I had ever heard.

'You have done what you have evidently been hesitating to do for some time.'

I frowned, her thoughts as difficult for me to grasp as dandelion seed on a summer breeze.

'You have already brought this young woman – Ffion – to life,' she explained. 'You have talked about her in such wonderful colour and vibrancy that she is already standing in front of me. She's laughing at the confusion on your face, and waiting for me to show her my latest painting. She's itching to walk down the road between the two of us, to listen to tales of your childhood and to smile at your funny ways.' Mother took my hand, something I couldn't recall her ever having done, even when I was small. 'She's around you and inside you and all you have to do is to let her be. She will walk by your side … as long as *you* continue to live *your* life.'

And with that she rose from the table, and headed for the door, leaving me to take Ffion by the hand and bring her back to life for myself.

Printed in Great Britain
by Amazon